PILGRIMS

GREAT PLACE BOOKS

PUBLISHED BY GREAT PLACE BOOKS
WWW.GREATPLACEBOOKS.COM
COPYRIGHT © 2025 DEVIN KELLY
ALL RIGHTS RESERVED

FIRST EDITION
GREAT PLACE BOOKS
CHICAGO, ILLINOIS
AUTHOR: DEVIN KELLY
LCCN: 2025942384
ISBN: 978-1-950987-59-7
DESIGNED BY AIDAN FITZGERALD
GPB 04

For my family
&
For every grace that has been offered to me

Remember how we used to wonder rather than know? We, wasted on the dawn, sickled over and over again; we, torpid, mal-equipped magicians...
— George Kovalenko

You would have to feel with me, else you would never know.
— George Eliot

Brother Keene

My brother ran away from home and never came back. He was sixteen. My dad was there when it happened, standing on a hill overlooking a field somewhere in Virginia, a field where once a thousand men charged across the space between one row of trees and another, and nine hundred men died.

According to my dad's account, my brother took off in the lead pack. He was a really good runner. Better than I ever was. In the *Post*, they ranked him as a "Runner to Watch" before the season began. There were only a few others. He was with that pack after the first mile, before they bent themselves into a single track trail through the woods, a trail where once—running against me—Dylan Johnson jammed his toe up against a rock and went headfirst into the root of a tree, his body prone on the ground as the other kids ran right over him.

My dad was at the mile marker the day my brother ran away. He was surrounded by a handful of coaches and parents. He hasn't seen my brother since. Later, they interviewed a runner—Marty Wells—who was in the lead pack with him. Marty was right behind my brother as they went into the woods, and then the trail veered left; my brother never turned. He ran straight through the bramble and kept on going. Marty yelled after my brother. He admitted later that the yell was halfhearted. *There was sweat in my throat,* he said. *I was like, what,* he said. He was the last person we know who saw my brother.

My dad recounted all of this to me. He told me about Marty Wells's halfhearted yell, and how the bramble opened to take my brother's body and closed right up behind him. That day, over the phone, my dad sounded so alone. Like someone telling a story about a bird that flew away. But not just any bird. A cardinal, maybe, that someone took a picture of as it bent its body to nibble the feed that someone had gently sprinkled along a porch's cast iron rail. A cardinal, eventually, that someone took to be a friend—a visitor from somewhere else. And then one day, no more. My dad sounded like that. Like someone fucked over by mystery. Mystery will do that. It will open some door far off in the distance, and close all the ones you can see.

What do I do now, my dad said.

You wait, I said. The word's out. There are people better than us at handling these things.

How can you not be worried, he said.

I am worried, I said.

It's because he's joined you, he said.

What?

He's joined you. First there was you, now there's both of you.

I held the phone away from my ear, feeling my dad's sadness grow into its old and familiar frustration. From somewhere in the back of my brain emerged an image of him on the other end of the phone: a bearded man, loose denim shirt, holding the phone with his left hand and, with his right, pulling a slot machine's lever one more time, that big huge slot machine of life; the machine was broken now, and when it once worked, he never felt he'd hit the jackpot.

I took that phone call from a wood-walled room inside a building with so many wood-walled rooms. I was a postulant then, in my year of candidacy at a Trappist abbey perched on a hill in upstate New York. When I talked to my dad, a great silence welled up around me, a silence that was always there. I held the phone back to my ear, and even then it was there. It was the silence of kitchens in dark houses, the silence of someone waking up to find something to eat, shuffling their feet so as not to wake anyone, stubbing a toe against the couch's wooden legs, muffling the noise from their mouth with a tired palm.

I am not lost, Dad, I said.

I know you're not lost, he said. But you're not here.

You're right. I am not there. I am here.

Here or there, he said. It doesn't matter. What matters is that you are away. And your brother is, too.

Away from what?

The world.

I am very much in the world.

You are in your world, he said. Not mine. Not anyone else's.

There are other people here.

I'm sure there are.

There was a pause. I felt my dad's sadness become a kind of anger.

And then I felt the anger go away. I felt it washed away by breath. And then there was more silence, and the sadness resumed. And then even more silence, and the sadness became weary. A big leaf drooping. And then we sat in the weariness, which was its own silence, except heavier, like we weren't holding phones, but rocks. And like we didn't know what to do with these rocks in our hands. So we just looked at them, each on our own. And then we set them down.

I'm sorry, he said. It's hard.

I know it's hard, I said.

Are you going to quote the Bible at me, he said.

When have I ever quoted the Bible at you?

I wondered about his choice of that little word: *at*. Little sharp thing it was. It sounded like *cat*. Or *scat*. Even *attack*. It sounded violent. And I wondered: *do I come across as violent? To anyone? To my father?* Strange—that such a tiny word could be so barbed. Though even a stab wound is just a little slit in the skin.

I know, he said, I just mean.

I could feel him quivering then, and he suddenly seemed old, so old. He seemed the kind of old you cannot reverse, which I guess is all forms of old, no matter what anyone says. He'd reached that point of oldness. And in his oldness he became small, and I thought he could maybe crawl through his end of the phone, cross the space between us, and emerge from my phone in the same room as me. But he didn't, because he couldn't. He was old and small and far away.

I know, I said. He will be found.

He will be found, he said.

I received that call on the communal phone at the abbey, in this room that felt purposely tucked away from everything else, as if it were a place where someone might keep a golden calf away from everyone if they had to keep a golden calf at all. The abbot beckoned me there and held out the phone like a foreign object, a diaper perhaps, something covered in shit. Though what would he know about that? When I hung up the phone, I was alone in the secret room, as I often found myself. Alone. In rooms. Some secret. Some not. Some of my own making. Some of the world's. And I sat there, knowing I would be undisturbed, and thought of my brother, all five-foot-eight-inches of him, all skin and bone, trudging through streams like some character out of the third edition of *Discovering Ourselves in Time: An Illustrated Early American History Textbook for High School Students*. I let myself imagine him identifying edible plants, figuring out which berry wouldn't kill him, even fashioning a small pickaxe out of the earthly things this earth provides. He was there in front of me, and we were together in our secret room, and he held out a berry to me that looked poisonous though I trusted him when he told me it wasn't. And then he was gone, and I lost the taste in my mouth. All of that—that image, that moment—lasted less than five seconds. And then I returned to simply knowing how it must be. My brother: young, despondent, alone, thinking that he was embarking on a mythical story, when really he was most likely enacting—a little bit too convincingly—some wayward fantasy of youth. And me? Then? I rose early at the sound of bells and mumbled my prayers. I spent my days baking, in the company of other prayerful bakers. I knew so much silence at that time that the sound of my father's voice had felt like a missile. A sorrowful missile moving in slow motion through the doldrums.

The following day I awoke in complete darkness, as I always had. Three in the morning. The moon was still in the sky, a little feverish and wobbly. I wandered, quiet and breathless, to our morning vigils. I held my not-yet-worn psalm book in my hand, murmuring myself awake in the back of the abbey's church. Up on the altar, Brother Olds droned on, perhaps not even awake yet. Though

I think he was. He had a voice fit for his name. It sounded ancient, as if the voice had traveled the long length of a subterranean tunnel to arrive at the end of the darkness that marked the opening that was his mouth. We made our way through the Book of Psalms.

What ailed thee, O thou sea, that thou fleddest?

When I heard that line, I felt myself catch. Or be caught, like someone yanked by an invisible string. I felt myself caught by something, yes. I don't want to say God. No, not yet. I'm not sure. Maybe I'll never be.

I didn't come to the abbey out of devotion to Christ. I came, instead, out of fear of the world. I wanted less of it and all its incessant beeping, how it so often took someone's eyes off the small joy of a dog doing that thing where it is breathing so hard it is kind of smiling and placed those eyes—without their permission—onto something else, a flash of ten million lights condensed into something so small it could fit in a pocket sewn inside a pocket. So I came to a place that had less. Though that's not the whole story. The whole story is longer, and involves my name, which I have revoked, and it involves fear, which I still have, and sadness, which I carry with me like a paper bag of groceries.

But sometimes, in my time at the abbey, I felt myself caught in this way. Caught by a line or a word or an image. Once, walking between the abbey's church and my room, I looked at the moon and then looked away and then looked at the moon again. And then I saw the moon droop just a little bit in the sky, like the woman tasked with the job of holding it up had grown tired, and let the yarn fall. But then the moon regained its presence. Shone above the trees. Relit the dark.

Don't worry, the moon said to me.

I know, I said.

What ailed thee, O thou sea, that thou fleddest?

And so, when I heard that line, I felt myself say, *God, are you there?*

God didn't answer. I think he was sleeping. I tried again. I said: *Is that you speaking to me?* And I thought maybe this is why we rose so early, to still be a little sheepish, a little less prepared and so more ready for God—all of their weird and wild ways. So that we might even say *yes, there's a little less I know and a whole lot more I don't.* Because instead of *sea*, I heard *brother*, and instead of *fleddest*, I heard *rannest the fuck away.*

What ailed thee, O brother, that thou rannest the fuck away?

We often went straight from vigils to breakfast, which was served communally in what one might imagine to be some kind of Gothic nave of long tables and holiness, but really resembled a late-century Denny's, somewhere between wood and Formica. That morning, though, I went straight from vigils to who knows where. It was still dark out, but the sky had arrived at that quality of, well, *morning*. There was some kind of light shimmering beneath the edges of the sky, like a stage lit from under its floorboards. The monastery was south of Rochester, not far from the Genesee River, and everything around it was flat lands and fields, roads that went on nearly forever. I knew the trees eventually ended. They always do, either at a road or a city or some distant shoreline. Nothing goes on forever.

I was at a Catholic university in New York City when I decided to visit the monastery for the first time. I confessed to a priest-professor my ever-rising sense of urgent malaise. I think that's what I called it: urgent malaise. I feared everything.

One day, leaving class, Stu Johnson—*Stooge*, people called him, deepening their voices and lengthening their vowels as they yelled his name from across the campus—touched me on the shoulder. He was a known person. Across social groups, across sports teams—everyone who was anyone knew him. Beloved and statuesque, he played the guitar each Tuesday night in the announcer's booth of the football field, a crowd of people gathered in the bleachers below him, each of them looking up toward him as he led them softly through a verse that built and built and built until it crescendoed into a foot-stomping shout.

Hey, the song went, *I was looking for my home.*

Hey, the song went, *and then I met you.*

Hey, the song went, *and I ain't looking for my home no more.*

Home, everyone sang together, *home home home.*

Yo, Stu said.

Hey, I said.

Beside us, all along the field that marked the center of campus, people from different companies sat in different tents, recruiting interns with free water bottles and promises of unpaid labor. I heard the word *network* a hundred times, and I felt disconnected and alone. Floating out in space.

What's your ten-year plan? Stu said.

My what, I said.

What's your ten-year plan? Your goals. I've been asking everyone.

I'm not a business major.

No problem, he said. Your life is a network. Now organize it.

Job. Wealth. Health. Relationships. Put them each in a column. Now tell me: in ten years, where are you at with each one?

I, I said.

It's not necessary—he touched me on the shoulder again—but it is necessary.

Behind the job fair, in the middle of the wide open green field, people sunbathed or tossed frisbees. Stu and I walked through a maze of suits. Someone handed me a pair of socks embroidered with dollar bills.

Free money, they said.

I tried not to take them, but it seemed I had to take them. I put them in my pocket, and fuzzy dollar bills peeked out.

So, Stu said. Your goals.

Okay, I said. Well, I still, I still don't really know.

Let me tell you some of mine. I want to run a marathon by the time I'm twenty-five. And then another marathon each year, each faster than the next until I'm thirty and people call me Mr. Fast. Like, I'm talking about people looking at me and knowing that I know how to endure some shit, and endure it *fastly*.

Fastly, I said.

Fastly, he said.

He smiled at this, and I tried to smile, too, but I did what I always do when I try to smile and can't—I looked down.

And, he said, that's what I'm viewing as my job. That's my job column. Serious stuff. Separately, I'll lock down a full-time hobby. Something in wealth management. I'll tackle that like a marathon.

Each year, I'll manage another million, another million, another million. Manage and grow.

How many millions are there in the world, I said.

There are at least a billion millions, he said.

And how many—

It's all exponential, he said.

And with his finger on my shoulder he drew a line that soared off my skin and into the air, until he was pointing at the sun. As he did this, we emerged from the job fair and had to walk around a tree breaking through the sidewalk, its gnarled trunk stretching for light.

It's not about how much or what's possible, he said. The world out there doesn't care. You have to believe in the limitless. You have to be as violent as the world is. You grow because you need to get big enough to answer its violence with your own. You grow big, baby. Big as a thundercloud.

But what if I don't—

It's winners and losers, bud.

I don't want to believe that.

No plan, Stu said, no life.

I watched someone chase a Frisbee down with a long, loping stride, bare feet touching the grass and then lifting off again. He soared into the air, leapt up to catch the disc, and just missed. I thought maybe he would cry, scream, slap the ground with his fist. But he just lay there, face down in the grass, and laughed a big belly laugh that made his whole body bounce. Once, after it snowed four feet one day in my childhood, my dad took me to the second floor of our house, bundled me in coats, and threw me out the window. I spread my arms, thinking them wings, and fell headlong into the winter dunes. My dad was there, seconds later, to grab me from the depths. My nose was red and my cheeks were red and my eyes stung so bad and we laughed so hard we cried.

I was a bird, I said then.

You were so bad at being a bird, he said. And you were so good, too.

What do you do, I thought, in a world that speaks in a language so different from that first one—that trying and failing and flailing language of being and becoming yourself?

Stu, I said, do you play guitar in your ten-year plan?

Do I play the guitar?

Yeah, is there—is there any part in your plan that talks about the guitar? And you playing it?

No, he said. I just love it. It doesn't belong in the plan. The plan is not about that.

Sure, I said. Yeah. I get it.

Speaking of. We're getting together above the field tonight. You know where. You'll come?

He slapped me on the shoulder and walked away. The Frisbee man was back to striding again. I moved past table after table of prospective employers, each arranging cards and papers at their respective places. There were so many of them out already. *What is this life*, I thought, and I didn't have an answer. I walked, then, to find Father Stilts.

Father Stilts was my priest-professor. He was, by his own admission, someone who had seen *Forrest Gump* too many times. He was one of those priests who had a *life before* the priesthood, and when I met him for office hours, he told me stories about this life. He did not withhold much. He smoked in that life before, and had girlfriends—even, once, a boyfriend—and he did various hard drugs that left him in various states of consciousness of which he remembered very little except where he would wake up. These stories often ended with him saying such a moment was *bad news* or *not great*. He eventually had enough bad news, and longed for better. He longed through theology classes and vows of silence and shifts on an oncology ward until he was there, sitting in front of me, with three stray cats he had collected from campus and a tattoo on his arm that quoted a question from one of Paul's letters: *Are your hearts tender and compassionate?*

I always feel nervous, Stilts, I said.

A symptom of your greater awareness, my friend.

Do you mean I will always feel nervous?

I mean, he said, yes.

I gripped the chair's arm, thinking of Stu sitting high above me in some building's top floor, then taking the elevator down for lunch and seeing me on the street—me, still trying to figure out what to make of my life in the midst of year six of his ten-year plan—and not even remembering my name.

Do you want to feel less than nervous?

I don't know what that means.

To accept your state of nervousness as part of who you are, to reframe it as a sign of your attention, and to live with it rather than to try to be apart from it—what do you make of that?

One of the cats walked a slow slalom between my legs and then fell to the ground and looked up at me with a scowl. I pet its belly with my foot while it attacked my shoe.

Another cat used one quick, sharp swipe of its paw to snag and snatch the pair of money socks that had been peeking out of my pocket.

I think I do accept my state of nervousness, I said. I just wish it wasn't the case.

Do other people anger you?

I just feel alone. It's like the world has said: *here I am*, and I don't like the world, and then the world says: *it is me or nothing*, and I don't want to choose nothing.

There's more, he said.

There's a brutality to life, I said. Maybe not life. But life, yeah. People want to attack it. Like, they really want to attack it. It all becomes work and warfare. Every employer—I gestured out of Stilts's window to the job fair below—is saying first year salary this, starting salary that. They promise more money in a year than I ever thought possible, and then I still bet when Stu or anyone gets that job, they'll complain about it all. They'll say what they say on campus when they're up late in the library. *This shit sucks me dry. This shit kills.* I want nothing of that world. It's so mean. But everyone lives in it.

Ah, he said. And then he coughed. And then he paused. And then he looked down at the cat still attacking my foot, and then at the cat mauling a pair of socks. Sometimes Father Stilts seemed like he was pretending to be somebody else, but then I remembered the stakes of his vow, and this life of renunciation he imposed on himself, and I felt a desperate admiration paired with a vague bewilderment in his presence.

The meanness of the world, he said. You know it exists alongside—and not in the absence of—peace? Let me tell you something. Once, I woke up handcuffed to a pipe in the green room of a music bar in Portland. A guy was screaming at me the moment I opened my eyes. He said I owed him two hundred bucks for a snare drum I had picked up and smashed my forehead through.

The meanness, I said.

Oh boy, he said. The meanness. That was not great. I don't know where it came from or why I did it, and I never will. But I will always remember that I did it. And maybe that I could again. I live with that meanness. And you know what?

Yeah?

My friend told me the next morning that I had tried to baptize a complete stranger's baby under a soda fountain.

The peace, I said.

The peace, my friend. You have to find yours.

I don't know how, I said.

It's not about knowing how, he said.

I looked down and saw that my shoelace had been, somehow and irrevocably, entirely removed from my shoe.

You know, he said, let me tell you something else.

You don't have to, I said. But I'll welcome it.

Once I woke up in a bathtub in a stranger's house in Seattle.

Not again, I said.

And I stared for maybe an hour at the tiles around the tub, and then at the grout between the tiles. It was orange, rust-like. Gross. Absolutely gross, brother. But there, probably in every house in America. And so I didn't know the house I was in, but I knew the grout. And that's all I knew about life. The grout. I didn't know anything else. Not my own home. Not my friends. I didn't know myself. I only knew the grout. I had read many books while sleeping on a mattress that sat on the bare wood of my bedroom floor. And I didn't know them, either. I knew then, finally, that if I wanted to know anything, which is part of loving something, I would have to change my life in a radical way.

Rilke, I said. You must change your life.

This was the only quote from Rilke I knew, and I used it often, mostly to myself. I'd walk around campus and look at the people and say *you must change your life*. But I wasn't talking to them. I wasn't even speaking out loud. I was talking to myself.

Yes, he said. I realized I must change my life.

And you did.

I did, he said. And you, friend?

Do I feel I must change my life? No. I just don't want to be so nervous.

I didn't tell him that I often walked around telling myself that I should change my life.

Well, he said, maybe you should consider someplace different. Someplace far different from this.

And with that, he told me about this monastery south of Rochester that accepted individuals to come out on their own for retreats. He sent an email on my behalf and a few days later, I found myself on a bus. Along grass highways. Beside long lakes. Through towns with factories and towns with one store, a post office, and a gas station clogged with bikers. I got off in Rochester and—because I still, after that bus ride, didn't know how to drive—walked the thirty miles to the monastery, my few days' worth of clothes riding in a pack high up on my back. I arrived, absolutely pouring sweat and devastated by thirst, and a monk batted not a single eyelash and showed me to my room, this bare bones thing without internet. From somewhere came the smell of bread.

I took one step outside and drew a deep breath. The sky was a blue, hazy thing, and even though the sun wasn't as bright and bold as it could be, the buildings on the monastery grounds glittered. Some were built from these dark rocks that speckled like constantly turning crystals, and the grass was wound through with paths that curved, it seemed, just for the sake of it. I didn't know if I was home, but I certainly wasn't in New York anymore. Whatever nervousness I still had was for an entirely different reason than anything I might call urgent malaise. I was just wondering if I was crazy.

I had been reading Thomas Merton's *The Seven Storey Mountain* on the way to Rochester. How many monks show up on their first day with that beefy book lodged in their pack? I'd bet two. At least two a year. I'd bet the number is higher for your everyday folks, which I was at the time, those just looking to get some monkish spirit on a weekend-long retreat. At one point in the book, Merton talks about his vocational godsend, this extraordinary moment that occurred in such an ordinary setting: eating breakfast with friends, a record on, pockets stuffed with cigarettes. He describes his desire to enter religious life as "a new and profound clear sense that this was what I really ought to do." On the bus, I underlined that passage and then looked out the window as we dropped off a cliff into Ithaca and then slowly climbed out of it until a massive lake emerged. I wanted that kind of clarity. I wanted it to be thrust into my life by a mighty hand punching down from the sky. I stared at the sky, but no hand came. The rocks only continued to glitter.

What I really ought to do. And what was that? Right before I left, I went into the newly-built business school to print an aimless theology paper, a final mess of words and ideas about this guy Karl Rahner, who, upon being asked if someone who wasn't a Christian could get into heaven, made up this term, *Anonymous Christian*, basically arguing that anyone could be welcomed into heaven if they were a good person. I wrote about how much I admired the idea but how it also felt a little overbearing to just label people as Christian even if they didn't ask for it. And so, I churned out pages and pages of how I basically felt a little weird about everything, and I went to print it all off at the newly-built business school, where the whole first floor was constructed as a replica of the New York Stock Exchange. A stock ticker ran the length of the wall.

That day, a crowd of business school kids gathered under the ticker as it threw these coded groups of letters and corresponding numbers and arrows across the room, the harsh neon of them illuminating the once boyish now slightly stubbled but still young and yet remarkably and uniformly chiseled faces of the students watching below. Everything inside was made of glass, so even though I was rooms away, I could see them there, gazing up as the numbers zoomed around and around. They were look-ing for something. Waiting. It seemed beatific. That was the word that came to mind as I counted the pages of my paper to make sure they all were there. Beatific. The crowd. The gazing. The green glow on the pale cheeks of the faces. The silence that sheltered me.

And then it happened. A once green arrow that pointed up turned red and immediately pointed down. And though I could not hear anything, I saw the mouths open and the arms go up. Something had happened. Something had been lost, and because of that loss, something had been won. And the students, eyes glittered with ambition, opened their wide and somehow beautiful mouths and opened them even further, and even wider. And their arms—pits free from sweat—reached skyward and touched shoulders on their way to God. And I saw Stu there, on the ground, his face gleaming as if just lotioned, glowing green and then, briefly, red. I looked at the pages I had printed, full of words like *predestination*, *risk*, and *faith*. And then I looked through the glass at the crowd. They were priests in suits.

I spent my three days of retreat at the monastery reading Merton. There are worse ways to spend one's time, I guess. And wandering. I did a lot of that. I ran, too. Like my brother, who at the time had just broken his middle school's mile record as an eighth grader, and who we—myself and my dad—assumed would etch his name into record books, would run a mile in a time that began with the number three.

Jim Ryun, my dad kept saying. He's going to be the next Jim Ryun.

And I'd think of Jim Ryun—hair cut close to his head, collarbones divoting his shoulders into shadows, running a world record on a dirt track somewhere in Kansas.

Jim Ryun, I'd say back. Jim Ryun.

On those three mornings, I woke to the sound of bells in what seemed like pitch black, though, when my eyes adjusted, it revealed itself as more of a blueblackpink, like someone had taken a soft pink watercolor brush and run it over gasoline. With nothing else to do, I would put on my running shoes, which I always triple knotted, untied, then triple knotted again, and jog down the monastery's cinder road until I found a path that ran along the river. I'd run until dawn became, well, dawn, and then turn back around and make my way toward that bare bones room. It was the smell of bread that would guide me back. By the end of my few days, I could've managed the way back in total darkness.

And it was that smell of bread I remembered the most when I returned to New York City, where sometimes the smell of bread would knock me senseless, how it snuck between the humid stink of dead rats and the bleachy exhaust of laundromats, reminding you of something good, like passing by the open door of an air-conditioned store on a hot summer day. It was hard not to be just a little romantic about it. I mean, yes, Jesus said something about man not living on bread alone, but it often seemed like living on bread alone could put you just a little bit closer to whatever you might think of as heaven. And making bread? That seemed right.

I spent my last morning of the retreat watching the monks make bread. It was not as romantic as I'd hoped. Though the walls of the monastery glittered like the eyes of a thousand old and wise men peering into the dark, the inside of the monastery didn't have the same allure. But the monks made a shit ton of bread. It was an operation. It got bagged and packaged and shipped off to, I imagine, those who might have, hooked by the novelty, once purchased a loaf of bread made by monks, only to find that, to their strange surprise, the loaf was quite good (and why wouldn't it be), and ordered a loaf again. And again. This consumption became part of their personal journey to salvation.

I watched these old baking monks shuffle from one massive machine to the next, gentle captains of industry. There was a kind of playful reverence to it, maybe enhanced by the minimal quality of the room they were in, which looked like something made only out of plywood and metal. If these guys weren't monks, I'd have thought them to just be old Italians. Little dudes playing these larger than life roles of tradition and culture, sometimes smiling, but mostly knowing exactly what their hands were supposed to do. You don't often get to witness someone doing something with a lot of love involved. But it happens every day. Every waking minute, someone is doing something somewhere, almost solely out of love. You have to decide to witness it, decide to pay attention to these acts—because it takes some looking before what seems ordinary becomes extraordinary. When it happens, when you see it—you look at something so small and notice the whole world churning to life inside of it.

Back at school, I realized how hard it was to find those moments of attention. Even my professors seemed somewhere else. I got A's on my papers just because they were long enough and contained an invisible prerequisite amount of properly punctuated compound sentences. The job fairs came and went, but I never attended. People left to go abroad and came back tanned, newly dressed, vaguely hungover.

One morning, after a group of students had succeeded in protesting the appearance on campus of a regressive and reductive political figure, I walked to class and passed a man with a microphone standing in front of a camera, interviewing random students about why they hated the person that they protested. Most students, oblivious, definitely hungover, couldn't put together an answer. Some students, I'm sure, could. But I watched the clip later—viral, already making its rounds—from the segment of the news organization's show that featured only the stammering of students who didn't know why they were being asked a question. Over and over again, the host called them idiots.

And still, throughout the days, I watched in silence from the glass-walled computer room of the business school as the glowing crowd screamed. *Fuck*, their mouths moved. *Yes*, their lips moved. And still that phrase—*what I really ought to do*—hung in the back of my head like a poster framed in the background of a bathroom mirror. The only routine I cherished was waking early on Friday mornings to walk to the bakery a few blocks away from the college bars, where once a week, they made only a few loaves of the richest, most delicious chocolate bread, these darkened balls of buttery dough still steaming from inside of the paper bag they bagged them in. I'd pull a loaf apart with my hands the moment I walked out of the shop, and the smell of chocolate mixed with the dewy scent of dawn as all around me trucks backed into the spaces next to restaurants and butchers and cheese shops, and people grinned and shouted and did the invisible dance of making the world a thing you can find pleasure in by the time the sun has crested the straight line of the horizon. I'd think, in those moments, *if this was my life*, and then the thought would stop there. Maybe that's what a vocation is. Just a simple decision to commit to eating chocolate bread.

As graduation loomed, I still had no idea what to do. The world was a place where, it seemed, everyone could be a baker, and almost no one was. The idea of the monastery was something wistful, a beautiful place I had once been, but nothing real—no part of a ten-year plan. And then it happened.

My man, Stu said, as he found me once more by the gnarled tree growing out of the sidewalk.

What's up, I said.

Tough luck, he said, gesturing at his phone before walking away, one single stride of his placing him almost out of sight.

And I sat down on a bench and took out my phone, which I kept on silent, and which was overflowing with Facebook notifications.

Go fuck yourself, messaged someone I had never met.

Fucking psycho killer—this, from another stranger.

Devil worshipping satanic fucker die die die in hell motherfucker.

I scrolled through it all, nearly delirious, wondering what had happened.

A stranger said: *I hope the breath you breathe while you're reading this is the last breath you take.*

And another: *Sicko monster fucker asshole I hope you die and then die again, but this time with a worse death than the one before.*

And again: *Your family should rot in hell too for giving birth to you, shitface.*

And then I saw the headline: *Disgruntled Employee Enters Walmart, Goes on Rampage, Kills Dozens.* His name, I noticed, was Bobby Keene. My name, I should tell you, is also Bobby Keene, but I don't call myself Bobby anymore.

Jesus, I said.

You are what's wrong with everything, someone said.

And then I began to cry.

I thought of what Stilts had said about the meanness and the peace, and how they existed alongside each other, and I wondered about the peace. I couldn't find it. I thought of being given something against my will, and not being able to say no. I was holding life in my hand, and I didn't like it. What is this, I wanted to say. Who are we, I wanted to say. Who am I.

All around me the world still moved. Someone was baking bread somewhere and someone was grieving and someone was turning their rage on someone they didn't know and someone was silently making a list of everything that was the worst about everything and someone was crossing one item off of their to-do list and someone was praying and someone was getting shot and someone was already taking a photo of something that happened and someone was sharing that photo and someone was receiving that photo and someone was saying *good god, what the fuck* and all the while someone was smiling somewhere, too, you have to believe it, but I was crying.

And then I turned my phone off, and threw it in the nearest trash can. It was all too much. The infinite scrolls of websites, the data points about the happiest countries in the world, the violence against people who were never given names by people whose names became, briefly, all we knew. The floor-to-ceiling windows. The endless glass. The suits. From inside the trash can, my phone beeped. It beeped and beeped and beeped.

The day after graduation, I boarded the bus to the monastery, trying once again to leave this world while staying in it.

And so, that morning after our collective vigils, I looked out into the dawn I had since gotten used to, and thought: *Well, this is my life.* I had committed to it after all. I was holding what I had been given, and it contained the dawn. Pink light around the dark world's edges.

My brother, in that same moment, must have been a small speck of boy running along a river. Maybe he wasn't fleeing. Maybe it was just his own calling. His own awkward, gangly-limbed calling. Not the greatest. Definitely unsafe. Extremely scary for everyone involved. But a calling nonetheless. And I: I was becoming a monk. I was supposed to be mustering a great and wide breadth of sympathy for all creatures on this planet twirling through the dark. And so I mustered it. I extended it to him. That poor kid. His name wasn't Jim Ryun. It was Billy Keene. And he is my brother.

Billy Keene

When I run, I feel like a god. A small god. Not a special one. Just one tasked with building some part of the world. In class, we learned about bureaucracies and efficiencies. We learned about the industrial revolution. We learned that there was a moment in time when people began to think of other people as machines. And so they delegated them tasks. That's the god I feel like when I run. A small-scale god. I have one little operation in one corner of the world. But it's my corner.

My dad is there at the start of every race. He is there silent like an Easter Island statue. The other dads are there and they are screaming and yelling. They are hurling all sorts of obscene words at their sons. But my dad is silent and he is my dad. I don't know what to make of this. He says he loves me at the end of each race. And when I win my race he says he is proud. Those are good words to hear. Love and proud. They are really nice to hear. But he has also hit me. He has hit before when he thinks I have done wrong, and I don't like that. I want to move through life knowing what I am supposed to do. Already I am older today than I was yesterday, but I know the same or even less. Or I know more and the more is not helping. It is a pain in the ass, the more.

Little dandelion field next to the start line. Little grass. Little person that I am. Little shit I know. Little scary shit that feels so big it is no longer little. Little scrawny legs are what I have. Little do I know, little do I know. Little flowers ahead of the painted line in the grass. Little wilderness about to be trampled by a thousand feet. Little is how far I go now, when I consider how far I might have to go later. Little thing that life sometimes feels. Little scratches I've made in journals when I've been supposed to be paying attention in class. Little poems written in the margins. Little house in the little doodle on the paper's other side. Little words that repeat themselves. Little the times I've not daydreamed. Little the life, big the dreams. Little do I know, though I want to. Little do I know, though I dream.

I stretch and shake my legs out. I wonder about winning. I think I will win, though this thinking does not change a thing. After each race I run, I return to being myself. For a small time I am a small god. I am a little scrawny thing flying around a field. I am a thing that comes in first. But then it ends, and my father says he's proud, and he takes me home, and we stop at McDonald's on the way. I eat a Double Quarter Pounder with Cheese and drink a soda that is all the possible sodas combined. DrPepperFantaCoca-ColaGingerAle. We sit down and watch ESPN until we know the score of every game that's ever been played. We don't say much. We say nothing. I wonder if he keeps the memory of hitting me the way I do—a burden in my chest, the bright yellow of the Tonka truck we never threw away caught in the corner of my eye as it happened, and now it lives there forever. A yellowness that could be love. My legs ache. My chest sometimes feels sore all day. I don't want a life of silence. I know that already. I want a life like a journal that everyone writes in. I want everyone's dreams. I want to know what we are all too scared to run away from. I want that bad. It hurts to hold life in. Life is really big. I am so small.

People know the cheetah is fast. But people do not know that every cheetah is so closely related that you can transplant a heart from one to the other without worrying about infection. You can transplant a lung, a kidney. One cheetah can be suffering and another can pull the heart out of its chest and sprint it toward the other before it dies, and put that heart into the other's chest. And nothing bad will happen. Nothing bad will happen at all.

I am fast enough to win. I am fast enough to run away from the rest of the field. I am fast enough to leave my feelings here, at the start line, while I go off to run alone. I am fast enough to sprint away from the mindfuck of memory. I am fast enough to run into a different version of myself. I am fast enough to make new memories. To un-keep the old. One doesn't rhyme with silver. The other is not gold. I am fast enough to turn my mind off and let my feet show me the way. I am fast enough to escape the prison of myself. I am fast enough to return before anyone has realized I was gone. I am fast enough to be loud in ways other than my voice. I am fast enough to hold pain in my heart and keep it there like someone spinning a bucket of paint around and around their head. I am fast enough to know the exact amount of suffering I am capable of suffering. I am fast enough to be tired for a longer distance than most. I am fast enough to run away.

I don't know, though I wonder. With what I know, I live. I don't know, though I wonder. With what I know, I live. I don't know, though I wonder. With what I know, I live. I don't know, though I wonder. With what I know, I live. I don't know, though I wonder. With what I know, I live. I don't know, though I wonder. With what I know, I live. I don't know, though I wonder. With what I know, I live. I don't know, though I wonder. With what I know, I live. I don't know, though I wonder. With what I know, I live. I don't know, though I wonder. With what I know, I live. I don't know, though I wonder. With what I know, I live. I don't know, though I wonder. With what I know, I live. I don't know, though I wonder. With what I know, I live. I don't know, though I wonder. With what I know, I live. I don't know, though I wonder. With what I know, I live.

I think of my mom, suddenly, before the race starts. I don't know much of her. She is like a vision. At school, I learned about the Shroud of Turin. My teacher projected the image onto the screen. I remember thinking it was like a cloud. It was like when you look at the sky and see in the sky the shape of something real. I think of my mom, suddenly, before the race starts. And it is like thinking of a cloud. It could be her. It could just be a cloud. I remember pancakes in the morning, a mess of batter in a bowl in the sink. There was a smell, and the smell was invisible, and when I remember the smell, I want there to be a body. Now there is nothing. I was so young when she left. I am still young now. I think I am old enough to start to think of the past differently. There is a world I think I could have had. You have to stop thinking about it. You just have to. You can't have it if you never did. I think of my mom, suddenly, before the race starts. She is reaching for me as she runs away. If that's not true, I can think it is.

When I run, I feel more than a little like a god. It's the power. It's the control. I know people can't control much. You're a liar if you say you can. The world goes on and the world keeps going on. There's a part of me that would like this if it didn't affect me so much. But I know that when I run, I can manage my breathing and my stride. I know that my heart can beat 170 times per minute for a very long time. I know that, when I am not exhausted, my heart can beat 170 times per minute while I run across a field at a pace faster than 5 minutes per mile. I know that I can sustain this effort. I can control it. I can tuck my pelvic bone under my spine and eat the earth with my legs. And I know that, when I devour the earth, I become a farmer making the ground new again so that different things can grow. We learned that, too, in one class. About the old ways of farming. People knew the earth a long time ago. That changed. No one screams about this these days. Everyone just goes on. No one seems to know the earth anymore. But when I run, I make the small bit of earth I am running on into a small bit of earth that is my own. In that patch of soil, I want good things to happen. Only good things. I want niceness. Kindness. No one is allowed to leave what they love. And everyone has to love. They must. That's how it works in my small corner of the earth. That's why I never want to leave and why the only way to stay is to keep running away. I am running and making this love so. When the gun goes off, I make this love so.

A Father's List of Things

three ticket stubs paperclipped together from a
Blue Jays-Red Sox game: July 17th, 2001
one expired passport, never used
forty mothballs on the closet floor
a blue suit, tailored for a child
sheet music for Don McLean's "American Pie"
two candles, never burnt
one log in the fireplace
one cookie jar that says *Cookie Jar*
specks of grease on the inside of the microwave
seven journals stacked atop a dresser
a tile uprooted from the kitchen floor
a note ripped from loose leaf paper that reads, simply,
turn on your inner light, my handsome man

Brother Keene

Years ago, when I was in college, I came back home and went for a run with my brother along a towpath that stretched the entire length of the C&O Canal. It was a soft path, flat miles forever. I used to run it alone on summer evenings, when the sun melted above the river, mellowed out and golden, dripping light. There was a spot a few miles north of the city where the trees along the canal disappeared, and if you looked left, you could see the river. Right there, in that spot, one tree stood, big enough to be seen from far off. It looked like two trees, not one, but it was one tree—one tree with a long branch twirling around it and extending outward. And it was wading in the water, this tree. It seemed to look out across the river.

People called it all sorts of things. They called it Twirl-a-Tree and Upright Boat. They called it Two Trees even though there was one, and they also called it Two Brothers. Or Two Sisters, depending on who you asked. The legend was that—sometime long ago—these two siblings went down to the water, determined to make some life for themselves on the other side. Things were bad on their side. The Civil War was raging and their dad was dead. Mom drank herself almost to death every night. They thought that somewhere on the other side of the river was a better world. They thought that because they were young, but also I think because they were human. And so the legend feels real. And they stood there for a long time, looking out together to the other side.

And one of the siblings walked out into the water. They kept saying *it's fine, it's fine, it's fine*. And they kept looking back at the sibling on the shore, whose arm was still held out as if they were holding someone. And then it wasn't fine, and the sibling in the water drowned. The legend says that the other sibling—the one who stayed on the shore—it says that they stood there forever until they became a tree, and their outstretched arm almost became another tree, wide and big enough to bring their lost love back into their embrace.

Running with my brother, I felt a bit out of practice. He, on the other hand, felt very much in practice. He was just starting high school, and full of movement and breath. When you run beside someone, you learn to listen to the cues their body communicates. You gauge the sharpness of their breathing, the calm or forced fall of their feet, and you understand how tired they are, or how much they have left in the proverbial tank. *Ponder the path of thy feet, and let all thy ways be established.* That's the Book of Proverbs. You can sense, though, when the person next to you is not yet pondering the path of their feet. When they are pondering, instead, the path of their body, and how much it has given, and how much it has yet to give, and how much it might be willing to give when the time for giving comes. I guess I mean that there's an energy. And that such energy is palpable.

As my brother continued to quicken the pace, I thought of those two trees in the water beside us. He dangled always a step ahead of me. I felt like the sibling on the shore, but still holding on, not yet relinquishing their brother to the water. Billy was like a horse who knew well enough to stay beside me, but also knew the intimate and yet grand allure of the racetrack. And if a horse wants to run, who are you to say no? It was as if he had aged spiritually in the time since I had seen him last. I know I sound like a monk. I am almost, in some ways, a monk. It was as if he had said to his life: *giddy the fuck up*. And then it did. It giddied the fuck up. And he became long-limbed despite being short. And cool under the constant pressure of effort. He became willing to walk out into the water.

You got fast, I said. Though I didn't really say it. I kind of grunted it.

I'm working on it, he said, barely breathing.

Dad makes me run with weights, he said.

Like literal dumbbells?

No, he said. He goes to the hardware store and buys these pipes and fills them with screws and stuff. And then he makes me hold them while I run.

You must get some weird looks.

I don't notice. It helps me keep my arms low. I know how to relax now. It helps.

I wish I knew how to do the same.

He didn't laugh, and I felt weirdly younger than him, like I was in the presence of someone who wasn't literally older than me, but perhaps was ages older in an esoteric way. I should say it blunt. I felt like I was running next to a monk. A gangly, pale-armed, light-footed monk. His eyes were fixed not at his shoes, as mine were when they were not eyeing him, but in the *inescapable middle distance*. That's a phrase from Faulkner. *Light in August*. In the novel, there's this wagon coming down the road, and it just lingers there, even though it's arriving, or not really arriving, just coming closer and closer, but not really. Like a suspended infinity. That's where my brother's eyes were. In a suspended infinity. It's how I imagined that one sibling looked while trying to walk the long water of the river. I imagine a forever-stare, the kind that sees no bounds, that only wants and wants and wants. And also knows. And knows. And knows.

We ran like that for miles, him breathlessly speeding up and me breathfully staying with him, sweat announcing itself to parts of my body that hadn't known sweat in for-seeming-ever. Had never needed to know. I wish I could say, after that run, that I felt closer to him. But I didn't. I felt so far away. There was still a silence between us, a silence filled with loss we didn't talk about. A mother gone and a father who raised us different. I felt like the wagon in Faulkner's novel. Or maybe the person looking at the wagon. And maybe the wagon was my brother. Really, I felt like the tree rooted in the water, its limb caught in a wild and strained reach across the river. Hoping for closeness, not finding it.

That whole run, I thought about what drives someone to look into the middle distance. People who look into distance itself, people who look through telescopes and who climb mountains and stand on top of them and look out across the land, people who spend an entire plane ride with their gaze affixed to the clouds—those people. Maybe they believe in hope. And those who zoom closer, who turn the microscope so it's zoomed close enough to see every smallest particle of dust and dirt and blood and body we inhale, maybe they believe only in what they know. But the middle distance—that space between: who looks there? He was so young when our mom left. I don't think he remembered what I remembered. But I don't know that. I don't know that at all. I only know the way both her hands clutched the car's wheel as I watched it pull away. And the way she didn't raise a single one of them. What distance was she staring into then? Close? Far? Middle? I remembered the long walks she took early in the day, how I'd see her coming back to the house, face painted with a thin film of sweat, a look of anxious energy that mustered itself into resolve as she neared. Maybe everyone has a moment when their life overflows. And the choice is either to drown or to stick your head in whatever looks like air. My brother might only know an absence. What is that like? To know nothing but know it should have been something?

On the bus ride back to the monastery for good, I put my forehead against the cold glass of the window and watched the world pass by. I thought of my mother then, and how I once woke up in the middle of the night and wandered through the house, not really knowing what I was looking for. I saw my mother then, sitting alone by the window, a glass of whiskey by her side, and her face pressed against the glass, either staring outward or staring at her reflection or both. I did the same thing on the bus. For an hour I'd watch the world outside, and for another hour I'd watch myself watching the world.

That bus ride was entirely empty save for me, the driver, and one passenger who boarded in Ithaca. Normally, I was a back-of-the-bus kind of person, but I didn't like the thought of so much empty space between me and the driver, so I sat near him. The other passenger sat in the back and groaned every time the bus bumped the slightest.

Fuckers, he kept saying.

After the fiftieth *fuckers*, the bus driver turned to me and my face pressed against the glass.

People will do anything but look at themselves, he said. Hell they'll look at photos of themselves but they won't look at themselves. They'll buy apples when they're not hungry and they'll let the apples rot. Do you understand?

I nodded. As I did, the tip of my nose cut a clear line through the fog my breath had made.

They'll scream out obscenities even on a Sunday and they'll say they didn't do it, and they'll blame someone, say they made them do it. Do you really understand?

I do, I said.

Fuckers, the guy in the back kept saying.

But you listen. You drive this bus long enough and you see people go and leave and then come back. You see someone pack one suitcase running away from their wife and then they're back on the bus a month later with the same clothes on, hoping she'll be where he left her. You see some people say they can't take the bullshit and then they smoke a cigarette at the next rest stop and they're crying on the phone apologizing to someone they didn't even know they hurt. Look, this is important. He slapped his hand hard against the giant steering wheel. I'm telling you. Do you understand?

One hundred percent, I said.

What I'm saying is that people run and run and run. They run and scream and yell. Every day. Every fucking day. I am the mouth that helps give voice to the yell. I am the ears that do the listening. I am the legs that do the running. People board me because they have to do whatever bullshit they feel they have to do. I once drove a man four hundred long miles across a state because he thought he left his oven on. Call it anxiety or call it honesty. What I am saying is that courage and fear are not the same thing. People say what a brave person to leave. They say what a scared person to leave. It's all bullshit, what people say. Only you know if you are brave. You have to look at yourself. People leave for all sorts of reasons. It's not all brave. They come back and realize they lost everything. But people leave, and you better hear me now, and then I never see them again. I think that means they did something brave. You hear me? They found love somewhere and then they stayed. It's okay to stay. Now that's what I'm trying to say. There's too many places to go. You've got to stay sometimes. You've got to find the love somewhere.

I didn't know how to thank him, and so I didn't. I got off the bus and walked the long miles to the monastery, and something began to feel possible.

Eventually, I had to work. The bakery shift began at sunrise. I took off my monk's uniform and donned the uniform of a monk who works at a bakery: this thin, white button-up. Pure anonymity. And then I left my bare, barely-lit room to walk the few minutes to the bakery as the sun shimmered the land to gold. It's funny. Try walking hard, with any sort of force, on a monastery. Like, really try. Try to jam your toes hard into the ground like a football player turning up the turf. You won't be able to. It's all soft footfall no matter what.

There were about eight of us in the kitchen, each with different roles. The loaves of bread took the least time. One of the brothers churned huge vats of dough before he poured the heaving mass into a machine that divided the wet, sticky flour into pans, which proofed before making their way along a belt that traveled into an oven, where they baked. It smelled fragrant, sweet, musky. At all times. Pure yeasty essence. It was beautiful. What could be better than bread?

I worked with a team of two others, making biscotti. All kinds. Walnut. Plain. Lemon. Chocolate. Brother Levine wore these big earmuffs as he fed uncut loaves of hard-packed biscotti into a slicer that sounded like ten million cicadas rising up from inside your body to make a home inside your eardrums. He was old, Levine was, and did his job carefully, with great precision. He had impeccable respect for the machine, which could slice your arm into a dozen perfectly cut segments. With his age, his faith, and his chosen profession, I think he felt the machine to be an extension of

God. Some sort of enactment of the fragility of life on earth. He treated it—this multi-bladed, steel slicer—with gentleness, knowing that, if he didn't, he would face a punishment for which there was no mercy. I never spoke with Brother Levine, but his presence soothed me. If God was the machine, Brother Levine was Saint Peter, benevolent and committed guarding God's gate. The one who stands beside the door and says *let me see if he is awake*, but knows he is asleep. All day long—feeding bread into the fractioned slit just above the floor.

It took me a long time to unwish myself from the bread. I wanted to be where the yeast was, to mush my hands into the vat and feel and smell the bacteria that keeps each of us alive. The beauty is there in the muck, but no one wants to see it. They smell the warm aftermath of loving work, work that runs its hands through all the stuff that sticks to a body. Working the biscotti line seemed like something lesser-than. What is biscotti but some mutant cookie, a glorified cracker, a tough and sharp thing that cuts the mouth? It *needs*. It *wants*. It is not enough on its own. It makes the teeth work, stretches the jaw too wide. It needs coffee to soften it, to make it tender enough to eat. Where is the soul in such a thing? Flavored and scattered through with nuts and dried fruit? Bread needs nothing. Bread is the body and soul as one, mixed together at their most vulnerable moment, and then warmed. When you are love itself, you don't have to be anything else.

It was Brother Levis who made me see it different. Brother Levis, who was in that ambiguous area between middle age and geriatricness, and whose name was eerily similar to his older, bread-baking monk-friend, a fact I never asked about, scared to rattle whatever invisible spirit-glue held the mystery of this place together. But Levis's age gave him a jocular quality. Enough life had passed for him not to be scared any longer of life itself. Death was too far away for him to give it his full attention. And so he did his job. He gathered the just-sliced biscotti into a messy pile and then slid the pile to me, which I arranged, calmly, with the non- urgency of someone who was committed to a life of simplicity, on a tray. I then took that tray and placed it into an oven for the biscotti to bake a second time and earn that sharp crunch for which it is known and for which it sometimes deserves to be softened. I spent a few hours every morning this way, hardly talking. Just arranging and baking, arranging and baking. Soon, there was something approaching pleasure in this work. We became one undercurrent of the world, a gentle rhythm that rocked against the baser frequencies.

The morning of the phone call, though, I felt distant, as if my body were somewhere beyond the bakery's walls, and my fingers touched not biscotti but something wet with dew. This resistance to stillness, this restlessness, a refusal to dwell in the *mysterious inner solitude* of Thomas Merton—it's the kind of feeling a monk will pick up on, if that monk happens to be standing next to you, day after day, for the better part of three hours.

Brother Levis saw it. I know he did, because I could feel, for the better part of an hour, his desire to speak about it. Brother Levine was no help, obsessed as he was with the machine of God. But Brother Levis stood a little closer to me. And his body hummed, too. A car radio that made no sound.

I noticed that much at least. And then he reached a hand over, just an inch. There was no biscotti in it. Just a hand, empty, waiting to be seen. I saw it.

This work has no point but stillness, Brother Levis said.

Then why do we move our hands so much, I said.

It's a stillness of the spirit, not the body, he said.

I'm not feeling that stillness today.

Yes. I can tell. There are some things that are not bearable.

Like stillness?

Like everything that is not stillness.

I see, I said.

He pushed the pile toward me, and I began to pluck one biscotti from the top, and then another, and then another, each time placing it on the tray beside me. They were perfect, arranged like the first professional sardines who were asked to lay themselves neatly in a can, and thus service the world for all of time with metaphor. I wanted to feel so immersed in my work, to feel nothing but what was bearable, but I could only think of my brother out there. It had been only a couple of hours since my father called. Was he running still? Had he stopped to take a break?

Brother Levis smiled. I didn't see his smile because I didn't turn to see it. But I sensed it. I sensed his smile. He was a big man. He could be radiant at times, like a cartoon sun peeking over a cartoon field. Before you can see its mouth, you know it's smiling.

You know, he said, when something bothers me, I like to invent a country in my mind.

What do you mean?

I do not create conditions for my existence. That is God's job. But I imagine myself among the conditions he has created that offer me the most joy.

Like trees?

Like trees, yes. But mostly I imagine a road, which, I know, seems more a condition created by man than God. But I allow myself that.

Where is the road going?

I don't imagine that. I simply put myself on the road. Big yellow lines painted down its middle. I walk upon those lines. I am in a clearing. There are trees everywhere, and most of the mountain has been climbed, but there is still some mountain left to go.

That offers you joy?

Yes. To be so far up, as if placed there, and to have some work to do, but not too much of it anymore. It's a climb that I can enjoy.

What do you think of?

Nothing, mostly. I simply am. It might sound funny from someone with a voice like mine. I know my voice sometimes sounds large, like a thing spoken from the inside of a bass drum. And I understand that I do not have the slightness that often presumes stillness. But I feel myself in the presence of something larger. Not some airy spirit, no. Just the mountain itself. It makes me feel small. I like that feeling. Because it makes this simple work we do—he gestured at the little mountain of biscotti—seem correct.

I think I understand, I said.

It is okay. I am not asking you to. You don't have to understand completely. Or at all. You are bothered, am I right?

I am bothered, I said.

Some people when they are bothered decide to leave. They leave whatever it is and wherever they are. They leave out of fear or anxiety or out of courage. They leave, and they are scared for their leaving, because leaving is scary. Even though the world is large and fast and full of potential homes, leaving is scary.

It is, I said, thinking if I had heard those words before—or some like them—as I held one biscotti between my thumb and forefinger and pawed the tip of a protruding almond with my fingernail.

Perhaps it is the largeness of the world that bothers you, he said. Perhaps you are insisting with your imagination a quality about the world that feels insurmountable. Maybe you should ask your imagination to insist on something less. Look at the largeness of the world. Give yourself over to it.

That feels hard.

It can be, he said.

And then he passed me a mountain of biscotti that he had made. I broke it down, little by little.

Being at the monastery offered moments such as that. You know, where you lived in a monastery and people spoke and the things they spoke would have sounded absolutely surreal and almost laughably spiritual if they were said in a world that was not a monastery. But we were in a monastery. People really talked like that. I don't know how else to say it. If, in some imagined future, someone said: *what was that like, your time in a monastery*, I would say: *it was like living in a monastery*.

After work, we had sext, which meant the *sixth* hour, not what you think it means. It mostly meant more psalms. My experience with psalms was almost always a kind of waiting. There was a lack of specificity in each verse that made listening to them feel like waking up on Christmas morning to a bunch of wrapped packages that each looked the same. You expected that similarity at all times, until you opened one and found something else. Maybe another box. A small one. Maybe a 2,000-piece puzzle. I listened and droned my own voice in congress with Brother Olds—whose voice was a cartoon train chugging along an endless track—and everyone else. And then I heard the line.

Examine me, O Lord, and prove me. Try my reins and my heart.

It didn't sound like my voice speaking. It sounded like my soul. I stood for the rest of the service and mouthed words I couldn't really hear. Maybe, in my imagined world, I was a horse. Maybe I had reins. I cared less about the rider, about who was holding the reins. That didn't matter at all. I could see the sun shimmer-shining on the mountains ahead, these jagged and beautiful things cloaked in grass and dirt and snow. And I was running toward it all, full tilt, heart beating out of my chest, feeling myself finally, for the first time, part of something *real*—the river beside me, the wind in my mane, the dust kicked up and floating toward outer space.

Back in the world I had left behind, I felt ridden at all times. Sometimes people climbed on my back uninvited. Sometimes they didn't even know they had climbed on my back. When Stu had asked about my plans and goals, it felt like I had to make a decision to become a part of a way of life that I had never asked to be considered for. Sometimes this felt like the very nature of someone like Stu's existence—to create a binary I simply had to accept. The things they would say. *It's your life. You've got to grab it. Make your destiny.* As if there was no other choice. I once walked past a massive, glass-walled, corporate building. I could see the people inside. Painted on the glass, in letters that were larger than me, was the phrase: *Take No Prisoners*. What kind of future, I thought, would that lead to? A future acquired by grabbing and making and taking? To take no prisoners literally means to kill the enemies. It means that there is an enemy, and that such an enemy—just randomly created out of the greedy headspace of a corporate imagination—should not be treated as a human. It means murder. What kind of future is that, where, instead of prisoners—an awful concept to begin with—there were just legions of discarded people, dead in the street, left to rot in the wake of all the grabbing and making and taking? In that narrative, though people thought they were giving others the reins, everyone was just competing for the same reins. The world was a big bucking horse, and a bunch of people wanted to tame it so that they could ride it for themselves.

I felt the psalm in my soul because I liked admitting that I had my own reins. Even more, I liked admitting I had a heart. Maybe, in some more beautiful world than this, reins wouldn't exist. But hearts, I think, definitely would.

Before my mom left, she gave me books of great beauty. Rilke's letters. Auden's collected. A bunch of Dickinson. She gave me anthologies of poems that haven't seen the light outside the narrow walls of a bookshelf in years. I didn't know she was leaving then. I thought maybe she wanted me to read all of them and get back to her. To crawl into bed like I used to as a kid and talk with her about them. So I did. I memorized Rilke writing *try to love the questions themselves.* And Auden, how he wrote that poem about the painting of Icarus, how he said that *everything turns away quite leisurely from the disaster.* He mentioned *important failures.* I didn't know what those were. Everything felt, to me, a little sad then. Failure was important because it fogged the room. I was ready to speak to my mom about these words, but then she left. She turned away from us all, didn't even raise a hand to say goodbye.

I held a grudge for a long time. I thought of those hands and how they didn't come up from the wheel to wave. I thought of all the words I still wanted to say. For a long time, I kept those words inside of me. I moved through life twisted shut.

One night, in college, my friend drank too much and I walked him home and he held onto my shoulder and staggered and stumbled. I took him to his room and we sat on the side of his bed and I rubbed his back and waited for him to throw up, but he never did. He tried to speak, but his voice was just a stammering thing. He looked like a costume of a ghost with the sheet removed—the same person, but different. It was as if, in not being able to think at all, he couldn't construct who he had been not long before. He wasn't there. That sheet was removed. He was just some feeling thing. A whimper under a mess of skin. He could only say *I'm sorry* over and over again, and he became sorry for so much, it seemed. For each *sorry* there was something attached. He was sorry for making me walk him home and sorry for his embarrassment and sorry for how I saw him like that and sorry for his appearance and sorry for caring about his appearance and sorry, too, for not being able to say anything other than that he was sorry.

When he finally fell asleep, and when I finally walked home, and when the once-busy streets were finally, at that time, quiet, I thought of my mom, and where there had been anger or just something silent, there was nothing. I no longer held a grudge. I no longer hold one. I don't know if such a thing is in my nature. All growing up has taught me is that most people have a decent enough reason for doing everything they do, even if their execution isn't the best. Or the timing. Even if the action feels wrong.

I wondered, as I left the chapel and faced my few hours of solitary leisure, if that's why my brother ran away. He was so young when Mom left. He is still so young. Maybe there was something he knew. But probably, I imagined, there was so much he didn't. *Try to love the questions themselves.* And how hard was that? To love the unanswerable? To love the not-yet-answered? Asking someone to love the questions themselves was another way of asking them to love life itself, which was, if you turned your gaze toward it and did not look away, mostly full of questions. Why are people like this? Why does the world seem to always turn toward disaster, and tilt in such a way that everyone alive turns away? It gets tiring to see the world and ask the world and imagine the world, and then live in that same world and be among so many people not seeing or not asking or not imagining. Though maybe they are. And maybe they're just not seeing or asking or imagining in the way you do. But even that. Even that is tiring. Maybe my brother ran away because he wanted only to see how it felt. No goodbyes, no nothing. The world as it is. His body in it.

I found myself staring again at the open fields splaying out and away from the monastery, waiting for the moon to say hello, even during daylight. Would a bird alight on my shoulder and say *everything will be okay, this is just the natural order of things*? Would a tree uproot itself, meander toward me, clap a big gnarled limb on my shoulder, and say *it's okay, my friend, hop on my back, let's go out there and find him*? I waited. I waited longer. No moon. No bird. No tree. Just the ten-thousand-fold choir of crickets becoming one single chirping sound and the occasional drone of a car making its way somewhere or leaving somewhere else. I needed to talk to someone. It was time to find the abbot.

Found Letter From Mother To Father

October 2nd, 1987

My little handsome man, we were so young when we first met. Do you ever think of that? I do. I can close my eyes right now—a dream dark, time machine skill I have—and see you there.

You are sitting alone at your sister's wedding. I am there with someone else. Look at you, sweet man. Handsome. I love that word. Handsome. You are it. And I am watching you. You are rubbing the sharp end of a knife on your thumb. I say: that bad, huh. Remember? I say: you must be having so much fun. And you try so hard not to laugh, but you laugh.

We feel older now, much older. I know we are still young! I know this! But hey, weird god in heaven, we feel old, don't we? And I know there is a life ahead of us, this big and wide and large thing that life is. But I think about how young we were when we met, and how much bigger and wider and larger life felt then. It felt like we were making the whole world each time we touched.

That's a superpower, isn't it? To make the world, over and over again, with each touch? Do you think we know what our love can do? We should remind ourselves. We're not too old for that. Sometimes I feel like I am the first person discovering the first ocean anyone has ever seen.

Here, one more time. I am closing my eyes. Dream dark time machine skill I have. And we are sitting on the roof of that first apartment in Brookline. We are looking into all the other windows, so many of them hazy and blue. You say look at all those people watching their televisions. You say we don't need a life like that. And here I go. I am about to do something. I jump out of your arms and stand with my arms out and yell THE WORLD IS MY TELEVISION! You're laughing so hard.

I loved that laugh. I still do. If it was liquid in a bottle, it would be deep ocean blue and sparkling. You've always been so small, my handsome man, but there is a laugh inside you that is huge.

I am writing this from my little room at the residency. It is by the ocean on the tippy tip of the Cape, and even now the only sound is the scratch scratch of my pen on this paper and the warm, soft gushing of the water as it washes up on shore. I don't feel as tired here. I don't feel like I need to wash away the lonelies with whiskey or wine. You remember that, don't you? When I started getting the lonelies. It felt like climbing up a ladder to the top of a building that was built only in my mind. And there was no sky up there. No stars. I know that word must have been hard to hear. Lonelies. I know it probably still is. To hear me, right next to you, tell you that I'm lonely. But you laughed the first time and called it the lonelies. That was something special you did there. Superpower of yours. Little skill you have. You found laughter in the empty treasure map of sadness that I was. Do you see what I mean about making the world? I felt lonely then, but also not at all.

I am trying to write my poems and make them good. They were easier to write when we were young. They sometimes flowed out of me like that water over there. That was me, pouring myself over the pages. But here, I write slower. Today I wrote:

The ocean puts the blue on the rocks
Like a child who wants to touch everything
& raises the toast to their face to lick the jelly off
A speck of sugar on the great cliff of the nose
Sometimes in my sadness I forget
The great bigness of what is little
& the tiny smallness of what feels large

It is lonely here, but it is a good lonely. I don't need to run away from it. And when I get too lonely, there is that image of you in the corner with the knife, trying so hard to seem serious, and so easily made un-serious. Let's keep it that way. Let's bet on it.

When I think of you, I think of you laughing. It's easy to do and makes you hear with me, the sound of you unbottled, joining the waves and filling the room. There we are, making the world again. I don't know if you'd love it here. You can be so serious sometimes, so determined. But know that when I think of you, I think of you laughing. I will be home soon, and we can laugh again. Let's try to laugh a thousand times.

Yours...

Brother Keene

Abbot Augustine was younger than most of the other monks at the monastery, but he appeared ancient from the first time I saw him. He had a shaved head. He was slight, barely there, as if his body had been slowly and surely whittled away by acts of grace that eroded him from the inside out. He was a man rustling himself out of a mountain that gave shade to the valley below. Little chunks of flesh, bits of skin falling from him as he moved through the world, offering what grace he could to each thing. Some grace for you, grass. Some grace for you, fellow man. Some grace for you, grace. Okay. To be in his presence was to make of the smallness of his body a kind of spiritual testament. His tiny stature meant he had a big soul.

He paused often as he spoke, holding a face that could've been a smile or could've been something meant to make you rethink your life without the help of words. It was hard to say. It made you pause. And what ended up happening was that any conversation you had with Abbot Augustine was mainly an exercise in silence. Maybe this is why he was an abbot and I was still trying to be a monk.

I found him in his office. It was as if he had been waiting for me. He definitely had not been waiting for me. He definitely had official abbot business to attend to. Choosing psalms for the day, tallying bread sales, cultivating ongoing relationships with the lay people of the surrounding, mostly unpopulated areas, coordinating the watering schedule of the plants, one of which was a fickle fiddle leaf fig that had been moved from foyer to foyer as it shed its wide, hardened leaves, ensuring the prime speckled quality of the glittering rocks that constructed our beautiful abode, thinking through various typefaces for the monthly *A Monk's Life* newsletter, communicating with other abbots about silence, and how it feels, and what it's been saying. But being in a monastery does charge every aspect of life, however simple, with a dose of meaning. It is so quiet that the sounds of footsteps travel further than the footsteps go. So, in that way, he had been waiting for me.

Brother Keene, he said.

Abbot Augustine, I said.

And then the silence. He gestured and I sat. And then more silence.

What brings you here, he said.

I, I said. And then stopped.

He nodded. And looked straight at me, holding that face. I looked back at it. The wrinkles around his eyes looked less like wrinkles and more like little tributaries flowing into the wide, white sea of each sclera.

I have a feeling, he said.

Yes, I said.

Do you remember, he said. And then paused. And then looked out the window where nothing miraculous was happening.

Do you remember our conversation when you were considering your vocation?

I do, mostly, I said. In parts. I remember parts.

You spoke about the world, he said.

I did. I had probably too many thoughts about the world.

He smiled. Almost laughed. I don't know if he ever laughed. It wasn't that he wasn't serious. It was just that he never seemed to laugh.

No such thing, he said. But I asked you about the mystery of yourself.

And if I had considered it, I said.

Yes, he said.

And you said something about a painting.

I did, he said. I said that the mystery of the self is the mystery of a painting. There are the materials used. There is the fine-combed brush, and there is the artist's technique, the grip of their fingers on the wood. There is the way, perhaps, that the artist smells the yellow on their fingertips before applying the brush to it. It is not a mystery, but it is. When everything combines to become something we call art, it becomes something unsayable. We name everything we can because we know, in the end, that we won't be able to name anything at all.

I remember that, I said. I remember the color yellow.

Yes, he said. The color yellow.

And I remember that I said I had not considered the mystery of myself. Or that I hadn't considered it much. Or often. I think I said it was a good question, and that I would think about it more. And that I would like to have the time and space to think about it.

There is a depth to consider. I sense one could consider such a thing for a long time.

I get that sense, too. Or I'm starting to.

When I say depth, he said, do you think of the ocean?

Yes, I said. Well, I'm thinking of the ocean now.

I see. I find that most people associate the ocean with the word depth. I say deepness, and people think of water. I think it is because it is an easy metaphor. We know the ocean is there, and we know that it is very deep. And maybe, even, we fear that deepness, because it can be scary, and then that fear makes such an association linger longer in our minds. And so when someone says depth, we think of it. Do you see what I mean?

Yes, I said. I do.

But thinking that way is limiting, don't you think? None of us have, I imagine, been to the deepest depth of the ocean. So we have to imagine that deepness. We might even need a metaphor for that. So to use such deepness as a way to consider the deep mystery of our soul, well, it gets us nowhere, right? It feels like lazy thinking. Like using an image of something powerful to excuse ourselves from thinking. We often give the illusion of consideration when really we are not considering anything at all.

I sat there, not knowing what to say. I didn't know if he was scolding me or scolding the world, myself included. I guess, in that sense, he was scolding me regardless. My best option felt like silence.

The phone call, Abbot Augustine said. You're here because of the phone call.

I am, I said.

And then, more silence. The Abbot's office was unadorned. There were some books on the shelves. Various titles. I didn't spot any Merton. The furniture was simply upholstered, like what I had encountered in my first dorm room. Wood-adjacent armrests. Cloth coverings for the pillows. A kind of roughened texture that still felt mass-produced. Looking out the window, I could see a sky that felt absolutely whole in its blue-ness. I thought of the Abbot's comment about a painting. What makes a sky a sky? How much work? And what are the parts? I realized I had been awake for so many hours, and that it wasn't even noon. And I realized, too, for a brief second, that my life would be like this forever: being awake for so long, and wondering how long, and wondering why. But maybe the point was that I would stop wondering about such things.

We don't often allow for such a thing to happen, the Abbot said. Letting the world outside this world intrude on the mystery of this world.

It's not the same world?

It is. Yes. You are correct. But we are called to be here, away from that world—which is also this world. We are trying, here, to respond to that call, because we feel that such a call is real.

Thomas Merton, I said. He talked about the artificial tension of society.

The Abbot didn't say anything. I continued.

I no longer felt the need to be tense because of artifice, I said. That's what he said.

Yes, he said.

Then why let me take the phone call from that world? Why not protect me from it? When I'm already here?

Because it was your father. Because he sounded scared. And because fear lives in every world.

He was, I said. It does.

I thought of him, then. My dad. It had been, at this point, what? How many long hours since my brother had run away? Five? Six? Seven? In those hours, my dad must not have slept. He must not have allowed himself the kind of contemplation that I allowed myself. The kind of work. The dwelling. The tree-looking and bread-making and moon-gazing and the all-around-wondering if the world would talk, just fucking talk, to me. No. He must've been frantic. Must have spent every second on the phone or by the phone or with the phone. Must have driven back to the course, walked through the woods where ~~Bobby~~ Wells last saw my brother. Must have stood amongst trees for a different reason or without considering their tree-ness, their ability to be part of something that we are also a part of. He must have wondered, as I did, but wondered in rage and fear and shame and hurt and anxiety and loss and so much else. Or maybe he didn't. Maybe he just hurt. And maybe he hid that hurt behind a car turned on, the radio loud, the television left running—the whole world talking except for him. I never once saw him scared. The day mom left, he turned back into the house and made me and Billy an open-faced grilled cheese topped with fried spam and ketchup. We gobbled those up and forgot, for a minute, that everything was not fine. Growing up, I thought maybe there was a moment when a switch turned, and you never felt afraid again, and you knew immediately how to sort the laundry by the proper colors and wash it at the proper temperature. I thought maybe no one ever taught you those things, that they just became innate. And yet, for a long time, I've washed my clothes in one big pile, running the water as cold as I can. Maybe there is only fear, and always fear, and simply our difficult ability to admit it or ignore it or think there is another side to it, a place where there is no fear.

I don't know what to do, I said.

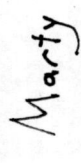

I have no job other than to advise you to do what you are called to do, he said.

And what if, I said.

There will always be what if, he said.

You didn't let me finish.

I did, he said. There will always be what if. Most of life is not knowing. Remember the ocean. To imagine the deepness is to accept with certainty the uncertainty of all his life. We can say we are always interrupted in the what if of our wondering, or we can say that we are forever in conversation with it all, and never interrupted.

I went to my room and took off my clothes. I folded my tunic and placed it in the bag I had been carrying when I arrived at the monastery. I had come wearing only a single outfit: a pair of jeans and a button down. My old, asphalt-burnt running shoes on my feet. I hadn't worn the jeans in months, and they felt odd, too tight. I wasn't used to being so touched, so constantly.

I don't know what I was planning to do. But I knew there was something I was planning to do. Some things are mysteries, I think. The heart is one of them. I had been alive, and in the midst of searching, and then a single phone call pointed my search toward something—or someone—else. I guess that's not a mystery. That happened. But the way it happens, and how it feels when it happens, and what it conjures up in your head—well, I guess that's the difference between being human and being nothing. Maybe mystery doesn't exist. But how we feel about what we don't know, that will always exist. And whether we say or do anything in response to that feeling at all.

I left my room and stood outside. The monastery felt small beside me. I wondered *is this enough to make a life?* Surely people had made do with smaller. Surely people still did. Surely people raised and still raise a family on a small patch of land, inside a small apartment, along a small street that contained only the few small things that might constitute a town. Surely people walked the same walk each day, drank the same coffee, replayed the same songs that they have known for years, songs that once exploded inside of them with wild, beautiful generosity but then became tiny, hard rocks—little crystals of memory and knowledge that they held onto for as long as they could. Surely people made do with smallness. Surely they still do. But in the other direction, where the trees extended before they ended, there was everything else. And in that everything was my brother, small as could be against the backdrop of it all.

When people thought small, they made do. When people thought big, they got lost. Maybe that's the history of everything.

In the copy of Auden's collected that she gave me, my mother wrote:

> *Little man, I hope that you have a life that is as big as this book. I know this book may seem smaller than life, but I think that it paints the picture of a life lived really big. Do you see how early he started writing? He never, never ever, stopped. Like a tank engine crawling up a hill. Like the sun coming up each morning. It gives me comfort, a comfort you might understand when you are older, to know that someone was trying to figure out a problem for a very long time. Life can be that: a problem. Believe me! But it can also be beautiful in its way. Did you know life can be both things at once? Both something ugly and something beautiful? I hope you have a life that is big in such a way, but is mostly full of beauty. I love you.*

She had dog-eared one page. Though maybe she had bought the book used, and someone else had dog-eared it. Either way, there was one page dog-eared. It was the poem about turning away from disaster. It began: *About suffering they were never wrong.* The poem described the fall of Icarus. Or rather, a painting of the fall of Icarus. It's a beautiful painting, a landscape of water. So much is happening. The farmer along the sea, the ships out to sail. The little community of life that shuffles itself together each day whether people are aware of it or not. The poems described the way, in the painting, some ordinary people—the farmer along the water, a horseman with his cart—turn away from this big, mythic thing, which seems a small and ordinary thing in the context of the painting: a small splash, a boy falling into the water. When I first read the poem, I thought about the people who had turned away, and I thought they were terrible for it. I wanted to shake them, to make them see that something had gone wrong, and that they could maybe help. But then I wondered about their lives. Sometimes a painting is more than just the colors inside the frame. Sometimes there is a whole world outside the frame. And there are families in that world, and love, and pain. Maybe people just have their minds on everything else. Their own lives and their own failures and their own little bits of suffering. Or big bits. Maybe these lives, their own lives, feel big and mythic to most people, and the stuff that becomes the stuff of legend feels, in the moment, too distant to even be relatable. Later, I looked it up, and saw that Auden had written that poem when he was young. A few years later, he wrote a poem that named how wrong we always seemed to be, how our stumbling was second nature, how we always suffered too little or too much. Maybe suffering was always on his mind. Maybe he was never wrong, because maybe there was too much to say. Maybe it's impossible to make a point. Maybe that was the point. All those people turned away from the boy falling into the water. All of them with so much on their minds. If the heart is a mystery, it is a distracting one.

You know, Brother Levis said, everything ends and begins in memory.

How did you get here, I said. Where did you come from?

You forget that I am a monk, Brother Levis said. I have my powers.

He smiled. His own tunic waved in the slight breeze sneaking up the hill. I got sad for a second, thinking of what it might be like to leave a place that a few people had come to out of desire to leave another place. Where in the world would you find such a thing? Maybe everywhere. The world was full of people who, thinking always of leaving, just stayed.

What do you mean, I said.

About being a monk with powers, he said. Or about memory?

About memory, I said.

Perhaps this is too secular of me. But I believe that everyone has a first moment, a moment of birth, you might say, when they realize that there was a point in their life when they might have done something differently. It's an origin story, you might say, a place from which to begin.

As he said this, the oak trees that lined the hillside bent almost horizontal, as if to tilt their old, scraggly faces to listen to a man who had just appeared. The crickets un-murmured themselves, bent their thin, stick-like legs, balanced on their pointed knees, and assumed a posture of silence. The rocks that held up the buildings where we made bread and prayed—they glittered.

And what do you do, Brother Levis said, with that beginning, which is also an end in and of itself? That, perhaps, is the ultimate question of life.

Do you have an origin story, I said.

When I was ten, my brother shot himself. He was fifteen. We hardly talked. We were in that period of childhood where things move so quickly. He had become so much closer to being a man in his own eyes than I had ever dreamed. For me, adulthood was the other end of a country. It was a revolution to be fought in a different decade. I was the only one home to hear the shot, which was an unfamiliar thing. It's only familiar to me now, that sound, because I have heard it once, and never again. And so it is still, perhaps, unfamiliar. I walked up the stairs saying his name. Though maybe I was only whispering it, and maybe not even whispering it at all. After I found his body, and sat beside it in silence, and cried, and sat even longer, and after my mother and father came home, and after they too found his body, and me beside it, and after they cried, and yelled, and screamed at my dead brother, and screamed, it seemed, over me, and at each other, and after the people came to take my brother away, and after the deep silence of that night, and the next day, and the next night, and after what felt like nothing, which is sometimes, I think, what grief feels like, I thought to myself: *maybe I should've done something.* You can tell me about how useless such a thought is, how little it will do to change what has already happened. Still. You can tell me such things. And even still. I might say that my life began there, in memory. I knew nothing about the world, and then I knew all of it. And I wanted to go back, to change what could not be changed. And I knew I couldn't. But I wanted to. And that wanting? It's the wanting that becomes the rest of life. Do you understand?

I'm so sorry, Brother Levis, I said.

I sit alone each day, he said. I sit among others but still alone. I work near you and walk among the trees and sometimes during the day we all become one voice out of the loneliness of each of our singular voices. I am as close, in this way, to mystery as I might ever be, which means I am as close as I can be to what cannot be found, which means, finally, that I am as close as I can be to my brother in that last moment before he decided he didn't want to be anyone any longer. If I cannot renew loss, I might as well live as loss does. In constant ritual.

And you'll never leave?

One day the silence will cut me loose, and I will keep on falling. And I will fall out of here and back into a world that I do not recognize. And then begin again. I do not say never though. I doubt. Doubt is why I am still here.

We stood together. The trees un-leaned themselves from the earth, bent back toward the sun. The world felt like everything and nothing at once. It was the blueness of the sky and the absence of the blue in what was not sky. It was remarkable, I thought, how you could spend a life trying to cultivate *a life*, and yet life itself, with all of its utter incomprehensibility, would shatter and break you, would say *and you thought you knew what this was*. What did I know? What did I know? In another lifetime, Thomas poked his own fingers through the holed hands of Christ. I always thought him to be one of the most human characters in that great, big book. He didn't do it because he doubted. He did it because he wanted to believe.

What do you think I should do, I said.

Rarely, Brother Levis said, do you get offered a chance to do something before you can say you should have done something. It seems you are about to leave. I can sense it in your heart. And you know what they say about the heart.

What do they say about the heart?

They say it is made of love.

The heart, I said, is just a heart. It moves the blood around.

Brother Levis looked at me. He had a big, wide face. If the Abbot's face was chiseled away by grace, Brother Levis's face was grace itself. A big, fat moon of it. A moon come down to earth.

The heart is never just a heart, he said. If it was, we would each know, at all times, exactly what to do.

I walked south in search of my brother. I had my pack on my back and my sneakers on my feet. I had a few packages of biscotti, and a loaf of bread. I had a wad of twenties that I emptied out of my checking account before I made the journey to the monastery. It might've been five hundred dollars. Twenty-five twenties. I wore jeans. I had no phone. It was in a trash can outside the bus station in Binghamton, where someone smoked two cigarettes, one in each hand. I felt more like a monk than I ever had, going back into the world like that. So limited. So constrained by the so little I had. Maybe, I thought, this was part of my vocation. It began with a phone call, didn't it? It began with something unexpected, the ordinary imploding itself, revealing the extraordinary underneath. Yes, maybe this was my calling. Maybe I was still a monk. And maybe this was a monk's mission: to walk in search of what might never be found.

At one point, Merton talks about being *back in the world*, with its *emptiness and futility and nothingness*. He's on a train, riding through industrial town after industrial town. But, at that point, he's so utterly consumed by his vocation that none of that bothers him. He's not compelled to *belong to it*. The world, that is. I remember reading that and wondering how that might feel—to see the world but feel so confident in your own small vocation within it that you no longer feel a part of it. That you feel part of the mystical, among the few who have created a world of their own. Maybe that's why people run away from home. When home betrays you, the world does too. They are one and the same. Home is simply the world in miniature. If that world, that small and intimate one, fails, then who would ever believe that the larger one wouldn't fail, either? And so you run, maybe. Not into the world that is outside home, but away from it. Away from belonging. Away from promises. Away from what happens when promises are not promises anymore. And you make your own promise, just with yourself. And when you do that, maybe you make a world.

I walked down River Road, which had no sidewalk and no lanes, just bare asphalt flanked by man-sized grass that did not seem to resemble corn. In Piffard, I stopped in a gas station that was just called THE BARN. They had PEACHES and HAMBURGERS and FISH FRY and BEEF ON WECK. All of these magical things, supposedly inside, spelled in massive letters on the building's street-facing wall. I only wanted a map. Before I entered, I walked past an old, rusting pickup truck with googly eyes pasted on the windshield.

Hi, I said to it.

A gentle, purring silence.

Inside, there were huge vats of peaches, and there was a counter with a menu above it, and on that menu were hamburgers, and fried fish, and beef on weck. I walked through the aisles looking for a map but found none. Then, near the register, I saw a wire rack that just said USED. On it sat ancient postcards written in ancient ink. I picked one up. A painted landscape. Letchworth State Park, the Grand Canyon of the East. Beautiful greens, a swirl of blue and white where the water cascaded through the canyon. On the back, there was a note:

Dear Phil,

You idiot! You should've come. Imagine: you, me, your arms around me, the water gushing through the trees. Instead, you're alone and I'm alone. I miss you, idiot love.

Yours,

Linda

P.S. I say it all in jest except the miss-you part.

P.S.S. Or do I? Idiot! You could've been here.

I put the card down. Everything on the rack was a single dollar. Next to the card there was an old AAA map of the Northeast. It was one of those things that folds inward 40 times and then folds out into a paper the size of a picnic table. I folded it out, found New York on the map, and saw that, through the exact place where I stood, someone had long-ago run a yellow highlighter down the length of a single road. The yellow strip began near Lake Erie and ended somewhere in Pennsylvania.

Thank you, I said to someone, though no one heard.

I looked at it again. The highlighted route reminded me, not in color or shape or due to anything remotely normal, of the Shroud of Turin—this thin, linen cloth bearing the faint image of Christ. Real or not, I imagine that whoever found it felt a tremor, a trembling at the mere sight of it, this reminder that wherever we are, at any time, has been ghosted, even gently, by those who have come before. I gave the man at the register a twenty and waited for my change.

You traveling, he said.

No, I said, just looking.

Just looking, he said.

Just looking, I said.

He made my change and held it in his hand and seemed to be about to give it to me, but then he squeezed real tight around the bills and coins until I looked at him. And then I looked at him. His face was so wrinkled that my first thought was to take a Q-Tip and slide it between the creases of his skin. Skin dust. Fairy dust. Bits of stuck world.

Just looking, he said.

I don't really know how to put it, I said.

The man seemed to squeeze harder around my twenty dollars minus one dollar minus tax. He would not relinquish my change.

Come with me, he said.

I followed this man who held my change tight in his fist. I followed him past the counter and past the fry station and out through a back door that opened into an asphalt lot. There was another man there. He was holding a carton that contained many cartons of milk. He was standing next to a truck that said BYRNE DAIRY.

Hi, he said to me. I'm Milkman.

The milkman, I said.

No, he said. I'm Milkman.

Milkman, the cash register man said, this person standing here bought a map. A used map. And then, when I asked him if he was going somewhere, he said he was just looking. Tell me. What do you make of that?

I don't know, Tom, Milkman said. Some people are just looking.

For what, Tom said. I don't look for nothing anymore.

Why don't you ask him?

Tom turned to me,

What are you looking for, he said.

I'm looking for someone who doesn't want to be found.

Ah, Tom said.

You see, Milkman said.

He told me, Tom said.

He did, Milkman said.

Yes, Tom said.

All you had to do was ask, Milkman said.

I asked, Tom said.

You did, Milkman said.

Hey Milkman, Tom said.

Yes, Milkman said.

A used map, Tom said. How about that? Someone returns a map. What do you think of that?

What do I think, Milkman said.

You think they found what they were looking for, Tom said. Or do you think they got lost again?

A question, Milkman said.

Tom turned to me. Then Milkman turned to me, too.

What do you think, Tom said.

I don't know, I said. I only bought it because I don't know where to start.

Let me answer this, Tom, Milkman said.

Okay, Tom said.

Alright, Milkman said. You're looking for someone who doesn't want to be found. That's like loving someone who doesn't want to be loved. It's all a mess in your head. Here, let me put this down.

He put down the milk.

I've been delivering milk for going on thirty years, Milkman said. It's a lot of time in a truck. I deliver milk here. I deliver milk there. I'm everywhere. Sometimes when I get in my head I start to see the traffic lights, the old red and green signals, and then I start thinking about signals all over the place. I start overthinking stop signs, start signs. I overthink my life. I think about my daughter, who—forgive me, stranger—I once yelled at because she came home drunk at thirteen, and I smelled the shit on her breath, and I didn't ask her about anything or try to see if she was okay. I just yelled and yelled and yelled. I said awful, bone-rattling shit. I threatened the collapse of high heaven. And sometimes at night, driving my rounds, seeing the signals turn from red to green and green to red, I think about her and I ask myself if she thinks about that. About that one night and about me yelling so loud I scared the moon into hiding behind Mars. Basically, what I'm saying is that I think about if she hates me. Eventually, I realized the only way forward was just to hold her close, tell her I love her. Do you see what I'm saying?

Tom nodded.

I nodded, too. Drivers everywhere were telling me things.

I got so used to confusing the signals, Milkman said, that I stopped listening to any of the signals at all.

So, I said, you're saying that I should love.

Yes, Milkman said. I'm saying that you should love.

You should love, Tom said. And then he handed me back my change. It was the same twenty I had given him, crumpled beyond belief.

Thanks, Milkman, I said. Thanks, Tom.

When I left, I wondered why it was my first impulse—when I saw this place, or any place with long grass peeking through its porch—to assume that nothing of worth might exist in such a place? To assume that the people inside would be as crooked as the roof that housed them? Would be out of touch with the spiritual, the sacred, the beautiful, and the trees? And if that was the case, why did I consider myself any different? Not crooked? Truly spiritual? In touch with the sacred. Me. Whose belongings entailed only some packaged bread made by monks. A map. Me, with no real plan for life at all? What did I know about love? I've left every home I've been offered.

I spread the map out on a picnic table. It depicted the entire Eastern seaboard north of Virginia. There was an axis running along each side. It went A-Z from left to right, and 1-50 from top to bottom. The yellow line ran diagonally across the map, southeast through New York. I decided to follow it. This was, I thought, how things happen. You stumble where others have stumbled, and hope that, in their stumbling, they have made you a path.

Billy Keene

I do not care for people. I do not care for people.

This is what I say, over and over again, as I run through the woods. Sometimes I make rules for myself with what I say. I say I can only talk to myself without repeating a word for five minutes straight. Not even a world like *the*. Or *a*. Or *I*. I want to make it even harder on myself. It goes like this:

Tree hangs wild like hair of tired lion. Brittle wood, soggy grass. Maybe it rained once, not long ago. Road in the far away distance. I can hear cars. They go *vroomvrooomvroom*, but really more rainy. Something about engines when sounding from long off. Almost soothing. Civilization near, still miles to go. White noise. Alarm bell that cannot wake you. First stars seen. Missing. Miss. Someone misses somewhere. Is it me?

I can live like this. I can live like this.

When I ran, I did that often. I let one phrase sit in my mind. I listened to it and made my feet fall to its sound. I did it over and over again, until I became the phrase. Sometimes, it was just one word. I remember hearing someone saying *trust yourself* to someone else on the race course, and I said that one word—*trust*—like a bass drum beneath the rhythm of my feet. *Trust trust trust trust trust*. I said it to myself and made one word land as my right foot landed and one word land as my left foot landed. I said each word faster and faster until I won the race. *Trust*, I said throughout the race. *Yourself*, I said the moment I finished.

I have found a trail and I will walk it. It is not too narrow, and sometimes full of rocks. But it is a trail. I have passed some structures that have roofs that seem to be for people on the trail. And now I am on the trail. So those structures are for me. I can live like this. I can live like this. When I stop, I will stop where a structure is, and I will sleep. I can live like this. And when I sleep, I will sleep like that. Safe and under a roof. Not much is different now. Just the stars, when I see them, and how they are brighter than before. They are bright like headlights coming toward me on a road. But I do not have to move away. I know they are as far away as they need to be. I can be safe when I look at them. I can move at my own pace.

In the morning when I wake there is what looks like smoke in between the trees. I think it is fog. Or steam. The daylight is just about to shine. Before it does it is soft like the pink underneath the skin of my palm. Pink fog, little mist. I like it like this. I am still wearing almost nothing. Short shorts, thin jersey. I must look like I look. Against the wall of the shelter there is a cardboard box. On it, someone has written *trail magic*. Trail magic. What place is this, where people might write such a thing? In the box are bits of clothes. A tattered jacket, sweats. Two pairs of shoes, one bigger than the other, both too big for me. I put the less big one on. I put the jacket on, too. The sweats. Don't need a mirror to know I look insane. The spigot in the ground gives water. I drink it and don't know who to thank. The trail goes in two directions. I pick one, and I walk.

Bristles bristle ankle hair. Hazy light becomes soft. Then warm. Later, maybe even blue. Branches pattern sky. If this is a season, I do not know which. Once again, one word sits in my mind. *Walk.* Remember running along long rivers. How old, me, no longer young? Prefrontal cortex. Developing brain. Big eyes for seeing. Singsong birds. Rustling beside. Brother always seemed so sad. Family, that word, strange thing. Wide sun burning. Hunger pain. Make it go away.

When the gun went off and I moved toward the front, I didn't know I would do this. I found my rhythm upon the grass, pulled beside the leaders. I ran with the pack through the first half mile, my gut tight. I had a feeling I would take the lead and that, when I did, I would not let it go. I took the lead just before the mile, on a low rise. I increased the rate of my steps, pushed my body up the hill, and put some distance between myself and the ones I left behind. Sometimes you can feel your body in the future. You can know the pain it will future-feel and agree to it in the present. When I turned into the woods, away from the crowd, I felt my body agree to something other than the race. I let myself follow myself. That's all. I felt myself being myself, and I allowed this. There was silence when I did this. And it is still silent now. It has been silent for a long time. I like it like that. Just my words and my rules. People say the heart is a lonely thing. I don't know. I have myself. That is something.

I heard somewhere that dolphins have to remind themselves to breathe. It's not automatic. It's not like me right now, breathing. I heard that dolphins have to think about taking each breath, and then they have to take it. I heard a captured dolphin once held its breath for so long that it died. They called it dolphin suicide. I have lost count of how many breaths I've taken today. I take so many. I think about so few.

I walk away. I walk alone. I walk because. I walk convinced. I walk contrived. I walk determined. I walk elephant. I walk fox. I walk forever. I walk going. I walk going. I walk gone. I walk horizon. I walk hungry. I walk inline. I walk insight. I walk jettisoned. I walk jangly. I walk keeling. I walk keeled. I walk lonesome. I walk lonely. I walk light. I walk mornings. I walk noon. I walk night. I walk only. I walk orangutan. I walk polluted. I walk pensive. I walk quizzical. I walk qualmed. I walk rigid. I walk rare. I walk skittish. I walk scared. I walk tired. I walk unwell. I walk unruly. I walk vivid. I walk vile. I walk walking. I walk xylophone. I walk yiddish. I walk zany. I walk.

I was upstairs when mother left. I was upstairs when brother did, too. Sometimes father would leave for a while, and I would be upstairs when he did. Sometimes, the best defense against departure is to separate yourself from it. Each time I waited a long time before I came down, and each time when I did, I was with myself. Alone. I'd run then. I'd put on my shoes and go down the middle of the street. Faster and faster each stride. I did not have to pretend I was running from anything, because everyone had already run from me. I liked to be free in that way, without choice, on the other side of choosing. When I followed my body into the woods, it was like that. Choiceless. I am sure someone is trying to find me. Does that mean I am lost? It does not feel that way. Here is the path. The path is where I walk.

Brother Keene

I've always loved the word *pilgrim*. I've loved the sound of it, the way it slips soft and inconsequentially from the tongue before hitting that hard detour of a g, which changes the sound of the remainder of the word. The word is like a cloak, light in the wind, yet draped heavy over the shoulders. You put it on, and you become as ordinary as a tree, a leaf in the wind and a root in the ground. I felt that way as I moved from place to place. Sometimes a car came rushing past. Big and loud and out of nowhere. There was the vast and empty silence, and then, in its place, a huge mechanical roar. A rush of wind. And then it was gone. I kept walking, feeling lesser than I was before, as if the car had taken a chunk of me with it, as if, with each step, I was being hollowed out by road and wind. I felt the lightness of the first half of *pilgrim*, and the heaviness of the second. I felt like a cup just poured out, and a cup waiting to be filled.

Once, Father Stilts told me about how he had tried to walk across the country.

I was in Seattle, he said. I didn't think much of life. I thought walking would help.

I thought of Ignatius, walking the long walk from his home in Loyola to Manresa. How must it have been, so long ago, to undertake such a journey, with a leg once shattered by a cannonball? So many hundreds of miles. Were people kinder then? Did they care less? More? Did they fear strangers? Did bad news travel slower? Did it travel at all? Is it possible to be a pilgrim now? Is there too much world, and so much more to avoid? In this world of speed, is there a speed so slow that it might as well make you invisible? My brother was out there somewhere, a pilgrim too. Would he call himself one?

Well, I said. Did it?

I didn't even pack a bag. I thought the world would help me.

Well, did it?

I remember leaving my apartment, and looking back at it. I made a long show of saying goodbye. I think I bowed.

Sitting there across from him, I bowed a bit, just to show him my own bow. The cats went on being cats, throwing silent scowls my way as my hair hung in front of my bent head.

And then I walked, he said. I walked for what seemed like such a long time. I got so hungry, brother. I reached a point where everything seemed unfamiliar.

How far away were you? From what you knew?

You have zero idea, he said. None. Zero. You might think I was forever away, but I was barely far at all. I must've walked ten miles. My feet were sore. The light, brother, was changing. And the cars were stopping for gas. I wanted a cigarette. It was bad news.

It wasn't like you were going to die, I said.

But that, my friend and brother, is not the point.

He scratched his head. I didn't know if he was bald or balding or just shaved his head on a relatively consistent basis. There was enough hair there that his scratching made a scratching sound. Sometimes he scratched his head and then bit his fingernails. He did that, then, in that moment. He scratched his head and bit his fingernails. One of the cats figure-eighted between his legs. Father Stilts looked like he was still thinking of walking away. His eyes were windowpane glass and somewhere behind them was his actual body, smaller and more full of longing, staring out at the world. Like he could go at any time.

No, he said, that wasn't the point. The point was that I was scared. Scared of how painful it felt, and so soon. And scared that there wasn't some easy answer. You know. Like in math, when you check your work and know the answer is right. And you sit up a little higher in your chair, thinking you're smarter than you are.

An easy answer to what?

To everything, brother. To big-fucking-everything. You know. A walk can't cure sadness. You feel that? A walk can't cure the world. I thought I'd get somewhere and I didn't think it would take time, and in the time I tried to get somewhere I only got far enough to see the sun hide behind an Exxon sign while I sat down and craved a smoke. No. A walk can't cure the world.

But maybe, I said. I don't know. Maybe—I don't know. Maybe it can offer, I don't know, maybe perspective? I don't know.

About what? Perspective about sameness? Unsameness? Changingness? Unchangingness? You can spend a day walking across a field, friend—

But you're still—

In a field. Yeah. Oh, buddy.

He scratched his head again. Bit his nails. Reached the same hand down to run a finger along the cat's spine.

I don't know, he said. I felt silly. I turned around, made it back home by night. That's when I realized I had said goodbye to my building, but never to my roommates. They just looked at me. Where you been, they said. I just said, out, like I had gone to look for drugs. Something I had done before. It would've made sense to them. That's when I felt more silly. Sillier. I thought I was doing something special, but it was so easily mistaken for something else.

I didn't say anything. I didn't know how many years ago that was, but here was Father Stilts, now *Father* Stilts, the same man, I guess, but also different. It was like a whole world could be held inside of someone. So many daytimes. So many nightfalls. So many new versions of the self inside the same old self. It was funny. What the world allowed and didn't allow. What the world made easy to understand about people, and what people, acting within the world, made hard to understand about themselves. I looked at Father Stilts and saw someone still scratching away at the sidewalk chalk painting of who he wanted to be.

Look, friend, Father Stilts said. I know the world seems big and scary to you. Fucking guess what? It is. The world is big and scary. That won't change. That will never change. The world is big and scary to me. I tried to walk across it and only made it a little way. Oh brother. When I found God, and stayed with God, it wasn't because God made the world any less big or any less scary. It was because God, as I understood the guy, seemed to know the world was big and scary. I think that's because he made it. Don't you think? Anyone who makes anything knows that sometimes it can get out of hand. Who do you think knows about plane crashes more than the person who built the plane? So I felt a little better in the hands of someone who knew what it was like to have things get a little out of hand. I still feel scared sometimes. I feel silly a lot. But at least I feel myself for such things. I don't have to feel ashamed. I used to feel ashamed of so much. You know what I mean, friend? I feel ashamed sometimes now. But I feel ashamed less.

I passed a billboard on the road that said *Have you sinned? Save yourself from HELL. Talk to Jesus NOW. Call (416) FOR-TRUTH.* I didn't have a phone. I don't know if I would have called if I did. But I imagined Jesus, stuck in a blank white room save for one inspirational poster, one with a photo of a bald eagle, wings outstretched over the Rockies, and the word COURAGE underneath it. I imagined him sitting in front of a phone that blinked red with thousands of waiting calls, each one pulsing to the beat of some tinny elevator music. I imagined him rehearsing his lines. *Jesus here... yes...I am the way...yes...the truth, too.* There were no windows in this room, just the eagle frozen in the frame. When he died, Jesus asked his dad *why*. Why have you forsaken me? *Forsaken*. That is a word unlike *pilgrim*. It is heavier. It is all heaviness. It rhymes, almost, with fate. There is a big weight to it. It acknowledges dependency. It claims no free will. Which is worse? Loneliness of one's choosing, or loneliness that comes after one has depended on someone else? What if the former is the result of the latter? Maybe it is just the loneliness that is the worst of all, no matter if you are in the call center or on the cross.

I walked. I walked for a long time. I snacked on biscotti and drank water from a bottle I filled inside a gas station's bathroom. I found shade in the dark square cast on the ground by the Sunoco sign, and I thought of Father Stilts. I unfolded the giant map. I was in a town named Savona, still in New York, still on the highlighted path. I was passed by cars going in both directions. I was a speck in the midst of everyone's great and big routine. There is a great and big world, and we are, for better or worse, part of it.

I walked past tall grass and little freckles of flowers. I walked past a store that was also a Post Office. I walked past two cats sunning themselves on a wood porch. I murmured under my breath: *Father Stilts, summon yourself and take these felines.* I walked past a row of plows unattached to cars, just waiting there for winter. I walked past a dumpster sitting on the side of the road, green and strong and unmoving and somehow still filled with trash. I walked past a sign that said DO YOU SOMETIMES GET HUNGRY? WELL NOW IS A GOOD TIME FOR THAT! TURN RIGHT FOR FRUIT. I wanted to turn right for fruit, but I was not going as fast as a car, so I walked a little longer and then turned right. There was a shed with a sign: SORRY, CLOSED. NO FRUIT TODAY.

I walked along a road in the high light of noon. The road was straight and long, and there was a brightness to the way the sun struck the white line threading the asphalt, and there was also a sadness, too. I thought of how hard it was to know how far you have gone when you don't know how far it is you're going. I was struck, almost instantly, by a memory of my brother and me, so many years ago. I was a kid; he was not much older than a baby. Our mother had put on a CD of Frank Sinatra's greatest hits. How she loved that old, big band stuff. The pomp and the brass. The richness of the sound. And my brother, who must have only been a few feet tall, kept holding an invisible microphone to his face and mouthing out words as if he was singing. Meanwhile the track would go on. *I've got you deep in the heart of me.* He would stop, sometimes, and strike a pose. *So deep in my heart, you're really a part of me.* And there he was—clear as day, so small, bare feet on the wooden floor—pretending at someone larger than himself. *I've got you under my skin.* Our mother thought it hilarious. She stood, framed by the doorway, trying so hard not to laugh, her hand pressed against her mouth, her fingers tickling her nose, and then she gave herself over to it. She doubled over. This boy surrounded by invisible trumpets, eyes closed, fake singing to high heaven.

I wondered, as I walked, if there was any part of her in that moment that couldn't believe this was her life. That couldn't believe that she had made this child, and that he was there in front of her, so full of soul, hearing the same music she had loved for so long. What a tragedy that you cannot live in a single moment of life for just a little longer than you do. That you can't pluck a memory from the past and go back to it, and stay there when the present gets too hard. That people get old, and leave the same rooms where they were once young. And then leave other rooms, too, and still more.

Found Letter From Mother To Father

February 3rd, 1993

Knock, knock. Hello? What post office is in between the room I am in and the room you are in, and does anybody work there? I am holding little Billy to my chest and writing this with my one free hand and you are in the next room and I don't know if I will send this to you. Hello? I am looking for the tiniest post office in the world. Even a little mouse would do. I would like to deliver a letter from me to you while we live in the same home. Tell me: who is the mailman working the roads between our hearts?

I will fold this up, then. I will keep it in our house and maybe let the words have a magic of their own. Little lamp of language—protect us all.

This little Billy, there is something about him. Bobby is so serious. He is asleep, too, in the other room. You know how he frowns while he sleeps? I find it adorable. Grumpy little man. Do you find it adorable, too? You, who are always frowning? I joke that he gets that resting scowl from you, but really this is not a joke. He gets that resting scowl from you.

I still have my secret skill, my dream dark time machine of magic. I am closing my eyes. And you are driving the car we are in, and we are by the beach, and Bobby is in the backseat? He has his arm out the window and you have no idea. You roll the window up and squeeze his arm so tight. He's crying. He's crying for so long, even after you roll the window back down. He puts his eyebrows together. He makes a great bridge of anger with them. It crosses his baby face. And you don't even apologize. You sit there driving and frowning but then, when I look at you, I see that you are crying too. You are crying silent tears by the ocean that is full of salt and your only son is in the backseat with big boy eyes of tears and your foot is on the gas and if there is an edge of the world you might drive us right off it. You don't say anything. And our brave boy in the back knows something is wrong, so he stops crying and tries to cheer you up. You, who hurt him not long before and still have not apologized. Hey. Do you remember this?

I am getting the lonelies again. They are taking the big world and making it so small. They are making it the world of you and these two boys, and I love everyone in this small world, but it is so small. I haven't written a poem in the longest time. I have piles of notes I rip in half and stuff into a coffee can. When you are at work, I walk outside with it and set it on fire, my little burning thing. Everyone must think I'm crazy. Wild. All day I chase the boys and feed the boys and stay with the boys. It is not so much tiring as it is no longer my life. I gave up my life to these little ones and now I live in their lives.

I guess I want to know: do you live here, too? You seem far away, a prince in your castle, always looking sternly at the papers you read and then litter by your feet. Always turning off and on the television. Remember me? Hello! The world is my television, and now there is a television in my world.

I don't mean to sound so sad. I love the boys. I love this little one by my body. He is so small and I want him to stay small forever. He is like a skinned peach, shining in the sun. Sometimes I put my mouth to his shoulder and explode my cheeks out and toot him like a horn and make him laugh. Growing up means meanness, and I don't want him to have that meanness. I want what is small and nice forever. I say it simply because it is simple. I don't sound like a poet anymore. I am losing that voice. I don't feel like the one who wrote about the spindly trees locked in their angry poses, yelling at us through the gnarled circles of their trunks:

> *Limb-locked and yelling, they say*
> *"Rescue us if you can, but if not we will*
> *force ourselves to learn how to love—*
> *stuck in the ground, we can still*
> *bend like maniacs toward the light."*

I guess I want to say: forgive me. Forgive me now. Forgive me early. Forgive me often. Forgive me later. When I pause in between the paragraphs, I reach for the glass of whiskey. I sip it over this bald, sleeping boy. The lonelies go away for a while. What happened to the world we said was ours? How did it get so small? And how can someone feel lonely in a place this tiny? When I reach for your laugh, I come up with only air. I am reaching still. I am reaching still. The road between our hearts is a highway. Postman, my tiny mouse darting between the rooms, if you are here, deliver this.

Yours...

A Father's List Of Things, Continued

a plane ticket—thick paper, faded by a decade: BOS to LGA
one single piano key, taken from a piano left out on the street
eight LEGO bricks, gathered in a coffee mug
a folded white oxford sheathed in thin gift wrap
dirty underwear by the bed
dirty socks, too
did you leave your laughter there, too?
your forgotten kindness, too?
a memory of one son helping the other touch a tree's bottom limb
four winter coats—yellow, yellow, blue, green—stuffed in a box
he lifted him up, didn't he?
five changed light bulbs sitting on the dresser, burnt out
like with his hands
an unopened invitation
he was holding him
three magnets for three pizza shops affixed to the fridge
and the other was reaching
the light in the morning falling through the window to the floor
he kept reaching like that
two eyes, waking up, that look away
and the other kept holding him up

Brother Keene

The yellow line took me to an asphalt lot by the side of the road. RACING, a sign said. DOGS, another sign said. There was a smattering of cars in the lot, and in the distance, a rinky-dink installation of bleachers. I walked toward them. There were maybe thirty people there, watching what seemed like bird-like blurs dart around a dirt track. Beyond the track was more grass, for what seemed like forever, and then a copse of trees that separated the grass from even more grass.

Beneath the bleachers, someone had set up a table. The table wore a sign that said BETS. Men walked up to it, and scowled at a few sheets of available paper, and then they pointed at something, mumbled something else, and handed over a roll of bills. I could feel the presence of dogs everywhere. I couldn't see them. But I could hear their high-pitched yelps in the distance, each yelp a yelp that made me know, almost instinctively, that they were thin.

I watched one race by the side of the track. The dogs were introduced by an announcer's dusty voice, the harsh grit of it crackling through the makeshift PA system, these speakers hung up on narrow wooden stakes, wires spanning the gap between them. They were in cages, the dogs were. Thin and bony and yet graceful—they looked like miniature figures trapped and spinning in an old jewelry box. When the gun went off, the dogs chased a stuffed rabbit affixed to a pole around the track. They chased so fast, tongues out, eyes wide and hopeless, the wind licking the skin of them in rippling waves. I wanted to cry.

Why, I thought, would my yellow line guide me here, to this place, where the dogs ran in circles but couldn't escape? The voice erupted through the speakers. The dogs ran as one long line of spit and sinew, eyes bulging as they each floated, four legs off the ground, for a brief second before ripping their paws through the dirt. When the race ended, I heard some scattered cheers, but mostly the silence of people cursing under their breath as they headed back toward the table under the bleachers.

To my right, I watched someone take one of the dogs, body heaving in such short, sharp bursts that I thought it might explode. He led the dog into a cage, and took the cage far off past the parking lot, where the cinder met the dirt, and further past that, where the dirt became brush and trees. He came back later with an empty cage. I felt a heaviness.

Maybe everywhere in this world it is possible to encounter the worst of us. Maybe the worst of us is not so much a different kind of person, but rather a way we choose to be, a way we could walk away from if we chose differently. I don't know. I couldn't be there anymore. I couldn't stomach it. I had to walk away.

Not even a mile down the road from the track, a car slowed to a stop next to me, then rolled its window down. As the crack grew, a dog's snout appeared, then its face, with its big wide eyes. The moment it saw me, though, the dog shrank back, and immediately there was a woman in its place. Mouth wide, hair all over the place. It seemed she had a smile caught in the midst of its widest possible position, held there forever.

Really, she said. You're out here walking? Just, like, here? For fun?

Yes, I said. Well, no.

This isn't real, she said. People don't actually do this. No one just walks—she took her hands off the wheel and gesticulated wildly—out here.

I could explain, I said. But I don't think the explaining would help.

I don't think it would either, she said. You're the one walking. You're the one being crazy, crazy man.

People have done crazier things.

Sure, she said. Just not in the wide fucking open. Most people keep their crazy to themselves.

That's probably true, I said.

I paused for a moment, looked at her, and then looked at all I could see of the dog—its ears making short, anxious circles. The car was this almost-SUV, battered a bit by weather. The paint chipped away above the tires. It was a dark green, marked by the occasional orange of where the rust cut through the cracks. That was pleasing to me. The orange cutting through the green.

And sad, I said.

Okay crazy, she said. Let's talk.

She reached over and popped the door open and the place where the dog once was—sitting all comfortable in the passenger seat—now existed as pure, empty space. The dog, quicker than any living thing had ever moved, had leapt to the car's back row. I climbed in.

You know, I said, I had it in my head that I would be walking awhile. I wanted to make this journey on foot.

You're testing me here, right? You're like Christ come from the dead? What journey? You won't tell me shit.

It's a lot—

You know, if you don't want the ride, you can just get out.

To tell—

And look. However far you've gone seems far. I don't know what rules you're playing by, but it doesn't hurt to break them.

Okay, I said.

I stayed in the car. She started it and it rumbled a bit before purring. She drove in the direction I'd been walking, covering what would've taken me minutes in seconds, hours in minutes. I looked back at the dog, who looked back at me with a stare that seemed at once curious and wildly forlorn. His chest rose and fell so quickly that I wondered how he'd even sucked in any air at all.

Did you race this dog, I said.

She slammed the brakes and her hair flew in front of her and then settled back in its place. She had been smiling, maybe in jest, with her whole face for the entirety of our short conversation, but now that same whole face was a wrinkling of confusion, a child's scribble of a dark pen against a blank page.

Race this dog, she said.

Sorry, I—

She started driving again, slowly. And she reached her hand back almost instinctively to find his fur, and her body became this two-pronged thing: half of her eyeing and driving down the road, the other slowing its hand into the tender touch of this breathing animal in the backseat.

This is Oslo, she said. At least, that's what I plan on calling him. I rescued this dog. Race? My god.

I looked back at him with the same curious gaze he had given me, and I saw what I hadn't seen before: little ribs, sharp and twisting, protruding like roots out of his body. A deep hollow around the eyes. I wanted to spoon feed him from a tub of applesauce. When I was a child, I used to use the foil lid of the individual-sized apple sauce container as a spoon. I curled it in my hand and dipped it in the sauce. Once, I raised it too quickly to my lips, and sliced slightly that part where both lips met and became my cheek.

Rescued from the track, I said. I was just there.

I stopped for a second. A silence hung in the air that was so palpable I wondered if certain nothings weighed more than certain everythings.

I didn't, I said, I didn't bet. It was just on my way. I just stopped there and left.

The greyhound track, she said. That makeshift piece of shit. Yes, rescued from there. I've got a whole house of rescues. I get word that a dog has lost a few races in a row, that he doesn't have a future, and I'm on the road as quick as can be. This bad boy is number six. It's a bit of a ragtag crew. Lovable losers. Not dead yet. They're all skittish and shy, but when you turn your head away, they run laps around the yard.

That's beautiful, I said. You're doing beautiful work.

I've never heard someone say the word beautiful twice in the span of a second.

It's a good word, I said.

Beautiful, I said to myself. It was a good word. It took three turns in the mouth, and fed you with the last one.

And what about you? Are you a rescue?

Is that why you stopped for me?

I looked at her after I asked. Her hair fell in these varied, burnt-brown spirals. Caught in the wind, it hung in the air and twirled like a field of wheat. She wore a denim shirt, and with one hand—she seemed to always be doing things with her hands—she reached into the bulge of her chest pocket to fish out a cigarette. She laughed as she lit it.

No, not at all, she said. I just think the world is funny.

The road seemed to glide along the landscape, and I thought of being in a cab once that drove along the East River. I had hailed it downtown and needed to go back up, and the lights of the city shimmered and danced on the river's surface the moment we turned around the city's southern point and zoomed beneath the bridges. I looked up to find specks of people walking across each one. Everything seemed so much faster than it was, but smoother, as if I had softened the anxious speed of the city by looking at it from behind a pane of magic glass. It felt a little bit like flying, like watching the world from a height that made everything seem not quite new, but gentle in miniature. I wanted to stay in that car forever, to have the driver race me in endless loops around the city, my fingers out the window, reaching for everything. Touching nothing.

You know, she said. You seem too tired to tell me anything.

I'm not tired, I said. Just thinking.

Sure, she said. Just thinking.

Just thinking, I said.

When I was a kid, she said, a kid sitting in the passenger seat, I'd put my head against the window and look at the clouds. And I'd come up with a name for each of the ones I saw. A complete nonsense name. Nothing that had ever existed before. Tangerinemachine. Uncleprettypants. Bustybobberoo. You see what I mean. And I'd be asleep in two minutes, guaranteed.

The clouds floated above me, the poofs of steamships sailing across the wide river of sky.

Scrambleddambledan. Bigeyesusiesue. Prettypinchofpeach.

When I woke up, I saw immediately that she was right about the dogs. You could see them from a distance, these soft streaks rushing against the backdrop of a little bungalow—one of those one-story homes with a tiny triangle on top where maybe an attic was. They were thin, gorgeous animals, almost like shortened horses, all the meat shorn from their bones. Curved and graceful, ampersands tilted over to the side. I wanted us to watch them from a distance forever. They could fit in the spaces between my hand's outstretched fingers. But soon, the car was pulling up to the house, and all the dogs—sure as she said—disappeared from view.

I feel terrible, I said. I don't know your name.

Patti, she said. Short for something longer.

Patti, I said. I've never met a Patti.

Well, now you have, she said.

She leaned forward and gently smashed her forehead into the wheel, cigarette still in her mouth. Took a drag, smoke in her face. She laughed.

What a dumb thing to say, she said, still laughing. She got out of the car and turned toward the back door, looking for Oslo.

And you, she said. Her voice a faceless and high and playful octave poking me from the backseat.

I froze, grateful she couldn't see me. I had been so used to forgoing my name, to simply being *Brother*. I had almost forgotten—maybe even more than almost—my name. And wasn't that what I wanted?

Keene, I said. Just Keene.

Just Keene, she said. Okay.

When she opened the back door, Oslo's behind slid away from the open door as if he had been pulled backward by the strongest hand holding the most invisible string. Patti didn't react. She just opened the door a little wider and began to murmur gently, a different kind of language, somewhere between music and words. As she did, she offered her hand slowly. There was all the care in the world, right there in that gesture. It could've lasted a few seconds or a few hours—the hand outstretched, the soft music from her mouth. I don't know. My head was turned toward it. I watched as Oslo unwound himself from that invisible string and moved his body toward Patti. I think all living things form trust easily at first. I don't know if it takes much. By the time we are conscious, the trust has already formed. I guess it can break quicker than that. But it can form. That part I know to be true. I watched. Soon, Oslo was a lump in Patti's arms, a fur-wrapped beating heart sitting right on top of hers. I followed her into the house.

So, she said later, as Oslo lapped cautiously from a bowl of water and I snuggled a coffee mug in both of my hands, Why are you walking down a two-lane road in the middle of nowhere, where the only inhabitants are people who rescue dogs and people who people need to be rescued from?

I don't have a driver's license, I said. And I'm trying to find my brother.

Is he lost? Do you live nearby?

Lost in a literal sense, maybe. Lost in a metaphorical sense, also maybe. I'm not sure.

Patti became exasperated. She lit another cigarette and leaned her chair back against the wall so it stood trepidatiously on its two hind legs. Her own legs went on the table.

Okay, she said. I'm assuming, at the very least, that he isn't found? That's what lost means, right?

And so I told her everything. I told her about Billy, and the race, and my father's phone call. I told her about Billy being out there, somewhere, among the trees and woods and who-knows-what. I told her about the glittering rocks and the mass-produced interiors. I told her about the monastery, and how I walked there, and about New York, and how I left there. I told her that I wasn't so sure about God but that I liked leaving the world, and I told her sometimes that I watched the moon when I got up early—so early, so very early—for our vigils. I told her about Brother Levine and Brother Levis. I didn't tell her about Brother Levis's brother, and how he found him, and how he holds that memory so close to his chest that it has become his chest. I didn't tell her how sad I sometimes got, being alone, or how sad I sometimes got, being surrounded by others, or how sad the world sometimes made me, in all of its incomprehensible bigness and big incomprehensibleness. I didn't tell her how sad I almost always felt, and how it was starting to feel like I might not have an answer for that feeling. I didn't tell her any of that.

Okay, Brother, she said. Brother Keene. A real live monk in my house. What did I do! To deserve! This! I feel like I should ask you for a blessing. Or ask you to bless my dogs. Can you bless away the rust from my car? Poor baby is getting old.

Please don't ask me for a blessing, I said. Though maybe I will bless your dogs. But it seems—are you ready for this? It seems they might have already found their blessing in you.

Oh, fuck you.

I forgive you for cursing.

Fuck you again.

The dogs began giddying up outside, in their sanctuary away from human contact, darting with hushed footfalls through the grass just beyond the walls. Sometimes a silence contains a heaviness and sometimes a silence is just the light emanating from a room you've walked into, a room where you no longer have to hide yourself.

You know, Patti said, I didn't think I'd get used to being alone, but I got used to being alone. When my husband left, it was before we ever had a kid, and there was a part of me—you know, out here—that felt this insane grief for a thing that never happened. I thought, well, if I don't have a kid with this guy, then there goes my last chance. And so I accepted loneliness, but it was a big fight. I mean, I really fought it. I'd drive to the bar twenty miles that way and sit there until it closed. You know, just to be around people. I liked that. I liked that it all would go on around me, and I could just sit there and listen. I didn't really want closeness. I just wanted, you know, closeness, I guess, but at a distance. I don't know if that makes sense.

It does, I said. Patti took her feet off the table and let her chair tilt back forward until it sat on all four legs. She talked to the window, and the window threw light on her face.

It does, I said.

And, you know, my mom would call and ask if I needed a visit, and I'd make something up. I'd say oh I would love one, but I'm too busy. I'm seeing someone. I'm seeing someone else. I'm working another job. I'm doing great. I'd make up something and then another thing and soon I told the story so many times that, well, okay fine, I'm not alone. I'm alone but I'm not. I'm fighting it but I'm still here. And I guess I just accepted it. And then I overheard someone at the bar talking about the dogs. I overheard them say something about shooting one of them out behind the track, and I got so mad but I swallowed that madness enough to turn and talk to this guy and ask him where and maybe could I go watch some races and he smiled and he told me where the races were and he told me where to find him if I wanted to find him, and the next night I just idled my car in the fairgrounds parking lot until I saw someone loading up their trailer with dogs and I took a big breath and went up to him and asked if he had any dog he didn't need, you know, any slow one, any old loser, because I knew a kid who wanted a dog, and he didn't say it nice or even warm, he just pointed at one, and that was the one I named Buzz, and, well, now I've got six of them so I guess I'm not really alone anymore.

Wow, I said.

That was a lot, I know, she said. I just had to say it. It's been a while since I said anything.

I hear you, I said.

It's just, she said.

A lot, I said.

You must be tired. I'll get you a blanket for that couch.

In the morning, I stood alone in the kitchen trying to find the light outside. There was barely any at all. I had gotten so used to waking in the dark, mumbling and fumbling my prayers. It was all moonglow and distant, lonely streetlight. A blueness above the country. I decided to make bread. I found the flour and salt. I found one of those packets of instant yeast and ripped it away from the others. I ran the water warm to the touch, and I mixed the water with the yeast until it bubbled and smelled a little pungent. Almost sweet. I remembered the smell. It came back to me, just like the moon. It hung there. Hello, moon. It smelled the smell that wafted up from the bowl and dangled in the room like dust in the light. It was that morning dark that is almost bright. That morning moon that is a quiet substitute for the sun. I made a hook with my right hand and circled it through the ball after I added the flour. I let it stick to my fingers as I moved my hand through the mass, and, as I did, I felt the mass become a mass. The shaggy dough on my fingers. I covered the bowl in a kitchen towel to let it rise, and I stepped outside.

My mom once went to rehab to get better. I didn't know it was called rehab at the time. I was young and my dad just told me she was sick. She told me that there was a small thing broken inside of her and that she had to fly somewhere far away so that it could be fixed by the people who fixed those things.

Will they be nice, I said.

The only person nicer is you, she said.

I hugged her and she did what she always did: she grabbed a fistful of my hair like a bouquet of flowers, and she leaned her face into it and took a deep breath.

Roses, she said.

Roses, I said.

She sent me a letter from rehab. In it, she wrote: *Look up at the sky and know that it's like a blanket that covers both of us, a blanket speckled with stars.* I was young enough to forget almost everything, but I never forgot that. I wondered where she was as I stood there. I wondered about my father. I wondered about Billy. Do the people we love know how much we think of them? Do we think of them enough? I tried to think about how often I thought of the people I loved. About the three of them: mom, dad, Billy. So much of life is lived in fear, knowing loss is on the horizon. Maybe closer. It's funny. It's on the horizon and then it's not. It travels faster than anything. Loss. You think it's slow, but it hangs in the distance for what feels like forever, and then it's right with you, right beside you in the present. That's one story of life. How quick loss happens. How far we try to keep it away.

There was the smell of smoke beside me, the crinkle-crackle sound of burning paper.

You're thinking of him, Patti said.

She stood beside me in plaid pajama bottoms and a zip-up hoodie, smoking a cigarette, her hair down. I noticed a few white strands caught up in the twirl of blonde and brown. She reminded me, even though I never really listened to Janis Joplin, of Janis Joplin.

Maybe I'm praying, I said.

Okay, she said. I'll be quiet.

She smiled with the sides of her mouth downturned, the kind of smile that makes sadness impossible.

We stood there in silence. Now and then, the slow burn and ember flare of Patti's cigarette. Out there in the distance was nothing but extended nothing. It was blue-black, approaching orange, but still dark. The stars had all left. The ground was a rich, textured shadow, its edges serrated by wisps of grass and the limbs of trees.

On top of this shadow was the sky's bigger shadow, growing lighter as the sun began to rise. It wasn't all that different from mornings at the monastery. It was even quieter. The dogs were asleep. There was no patient shuffling, no sound of a gentle herd of men moving from their own individual rooms to a big communal room where they would pray together. I didn't think of myself as praying, standing there beside Patti, but maybe I was.

A psalm echoed quietly from the sky down to me, as if I had never left.

For I am ready to halt, and my sorrow is continually before me.

Why did it seem like the person saying such a thing was acknowledging a life of absolute desperation? And then it came back to me.

What ailed thee, o sea, that thou fleddest? What ailed thee, o brother, that thou runnest away?

Years older than my brother, I knew nothing more than him. He was a kid, yes, but maybe he understood the world better than I did. I was always running away, too.

The thing was, I didn't know what ailed him. I knew what ailed me. At least, I think I did. I knew I was looking for a world of cosmic security. A world where people didn't just up and leave, where people didn't hustle around for no reason. I wanted a world of calm, a world where no one was going anywhere because there wasn't really anywhere to go. I wanted a world where the wondering was enough, where questions didn't always have to become answers, where no one tried to stamp the authority of certainty—a ten-year plan, numbers cascading around a room—over anyone's head, and make them escape into it rather than let them stay where they are, a mess of love and uncertainty and confusion and all the complicated shit that makes up a life.

I thought Billy was too young to understand something like

that. But maybe that's wrong. When I still slept in the same room as him, light years older than he was, I used to put him back into bed. He'd fall out in the middle of the night. Bad dreams. Awful terrors. I'd wake at the *thump* of his body rolling off the bed and hitting the floor. And I'd get out of bed, lift his little body in my arms. I'd put him back to sleep. Most times he wouldn't stir. One time, he did.

Why are you holding me, he said.

You fell, I said. You fell out the bed.

No I didn't. You're carrying me. You lifted me out.

I'm sorry, I said. You fell.

His face scrunched up, like he was thinking of the most serious answer to the world's hardest question. He was so light in my arms.

I'm helping you, I said.

But I didn't ask for it, he said.

That's because you were asleep, I said.

But if I fell, he said, I would have known it. I would have felt it.

I looked at him then and what I saw was a boy. I was a boy, too. We both were. We were small, and we were caught up among all the other small things in the great big thing we called the world. What did we know?

We don't know everything, I said. We can't.

But—

And then he drifted back to sleep.

What do you do in that situation other than carry someone back to bed?

Are you still praying, Patti said.

No, I said. I'm done.

She tossed her cigarette into a flower pot and lit another. The sun was inching its way above the horizon. Soon, we would be bathed in light.

I could use a prayer, she said.

I don't know one.

That's a lie.

I'm not some prayer generator. You can't just spin my wheel and be rewarded with God.

So you don't believe?

I don't not believe.

But if you believed, she said, you'd offer me a prayer.

She was doing that smile-thing again. With anyone else, I might call it a smirk, but with her, it seemed she was throwing a haymaker at sadness.

Not completely true, I said.

Okay, she said. Well. Give me something.

Look, I said, I want to believe. In something. Anything. I know I can be judgmental. Harsh, even. I left the city because there was so much I hated, and then, thinking back on it now, I hate how much I hated. I don't know if hate is a way to find God, or faith, or anything. But that's what I tried to do. And I think I hate a little less now, and search a little more.

Is that a prayer, Patti said.

I don't think so. I think I'm just complaining.

The light made its slow, wide advance across the grass.

I can try a prayer, Patti said.

Okay, I said.

She took a large drag and then a big exhale. She zipped up her sweater all the way and put her legs together and made the sign of the cross toward my body.

Is that fine, she said, smiling.

Perfect, I said.

She turned and made the sign of the cross toward the sun, toward the sleeping dogs, toward the morning light on the grass.

Bless the dogs, she said. And bless their skinny bodies. Bless their snouts and bless the things they smell. Bless us, too, but bless us last, and bless you more than me. Bless the lonely people, lonely all night. Bless the dogs most of all. Bless them enough so they get strong again. Let them run around for nothing. Bless fun. Bless the worst in us and bless the best. Bless what no one asked to be blessed.

I smiled so hard I almost cried. The sun was a blaze of glory on the horizon, and I was a kid, holding my brother's body in the night, not knowing who would leave and why. Not knowing anything about that at all.

How was that, Patti said.

Perfect, I said.

Do you love your brother?

I'd never thought about that until she asked.

I think I do, I said. When I think of him out there I want to reach my arms out longer than they can go. I want to find him.

If you could stretch your arm to touch my car from where you're standing, I'd sell my house and give my life to Jesus.

Let me try, I said.

I tried, and I failed.

So, she said, do you love your brother?

I do. I just have never said it. It's weird to admit it to someone else before I admit it to him. I want to find him and tell him that I love him. I want that love to make whatever is not okay okay. I don't know who he is. I don't know if he doubts or if he loves or if he's scared or if he's free.

Patti took a drag. The morning sun cast a purple-pink haze over the soft green of the grass that surrounded her house.

My grandma lived here before she died, she said. She sat all day on the couch where you slept. Sometimes she murmured little things. She'd start naming all these people I didn't know. She'd be talking to them. Margaret, I won't forget to call. Mary, here's my money for the collection plate if I can't make it to church. It was like she was trying to tie up the bow of life before it all got away from her. I guess I was hearing her die. And then she died, and none of those bows were tied.

Back at the monastery, Brother Levis was doing the work of

two people, gathering the biscotti into a pile and then arranging the pile back down into a tray. He was doing it kindly, maybe even smiling or murmuring to himself, not even thinking about the extra work. Not even thinking about his dead brother. He was just doing the work. Existing within it. Back home, my dad was waking up, walking little half-laps around the bed, shuffling through the piles of dirty laundry, scratching his face, wondering and worrying, putting his clothes on and then taking them off and then putting them back on again. He was going out to the car, opening the driver's side door, and sitting in it—key in the ignition, unturned. He was sitting there for a long time. Minutes becoming hours. He was not driving anywhere, not knowing where *where* was. Back in New York City, the bakery was laying out its few loaves of chocolate bread to sell, and the smell was wafting up from the corner of Hughes and 186th, and rising into the apartment windows above, where people still slept or were about to wake or had just woken up or had long since gone. And some people were coming home hours past midnight, not even drunk anymore, and others were holed up in their cubicles thirty, forty, fifty stories above the city, these little fluorescent squares of light anyone could see if they just bothered to look up. And none of it was normal and all of it was. And here, somewhere in the same state, in a palace that could be anywhere at all, awash in the pink light of morning that was shadowed by the tall grass, Patti was counting the dogs to make sure they were all alright, and as each one woke, it began to run.

Billy Keene

Rocks crooked, boulders jagged. Little bits of moss growing atop the stones. Like anyone, I can also trip. Have fallen. Will fall. Too much looking up does do you like that. Sometimes people pass. Kinda weird, to be seen. But not. They don't gaze twice. Only once. Guess everyone seems so secretly bonkers. White blazes painted on trees. Following long. Pipes pump water. Tired is life. Birdcall. Mating season. Gathering nuts. Fat winter. Pesky soul. What's a dream?

I need a new name. We need new names. I need a new name. We need new names.

I fall in with a group. They introduce themselves as Doctor, Whaleman, and High Five. I ask them their real names. They say those are them. They say you get a new name the longer you live out here. They ask me if I have one. I say no. I could have said yes. I could have called myself Maverick or Soft Serve or Big Bug. Instead I say I am nameless. They all nod or smile. They poke rocks with their toes. They seem to understand.

Once, I ran away from home. I was just a kid. I still am. I packed a paper bag with a banana and held it like a baton. I thought I would figure out food sometime later. I didn't make it far. I sprinted too fast. One block, then another, then another, then I was at the park and sitting on the bleachers, watching kids my age play baseball while their dads cheered them on. I ate the banana, not even famished, just not wanting it to waste. I walked home. Empty. No one was there when I left. No one there still. Sometimes what seem like big events are just little things we do.

They share their food with me. They fill a pot with water and fill the water with instant ramen and fill it still with powdered mashed potatoes. They put the pot on a camping stove. Ramen bomb, they say, and smile. The fire lights their faces and then shadows them. My mouth is a heap of salt. I am cold. I am gifted a sweater for my troubles. They ask me where I started. Georgia, they say, then wait. I say no. Not far from here. They ask if it's my first time. They don't tell me I look young. I share a tent with Doctor. He falls asleep humming "Country Roads."

This is my life now. This is my life now.

No verbs this time. Just trees. Just trails. Just someone scared of snakes. Morning dark. Whites of eyes. Folded tents. Big bags. Grumbling hours. At the ready. No words. Step after step after step. A cracked joke. Laughter. Sunlight through the branches. Sweater around my waist. Granola crunch. Dried cranberries. A life like this. History test. Failed grades. Unbrushed teeth. A stink in my mouth. A stink in my pits. A stink between my legs. No mind. And finally: words. Jumbled talk. Bits of story. Me, at the back. If a race, then what? If not?

Whaleman is whaleman because he once told a story about how much he loves whales. Really fucking much, he is said to have said. On the trail, he talks nonstop about orcas, big blues, finbacks, belugas. He says the finback is the loudest mammal on earth. He says a finback whale hanging out off the coast of New York can say hello to a finback hanging out off the coast of England. He says sound travels faster underwater because of the way water is. He says it so simply that it must be true. He says a baby blue whale grows eight pounds every second during its first year of life. He says you could be chomping away at it and you wouldn't even make a dent. High Five says why would you chomp away at a baby blue whale, are you a maniac, but Whaleman doesn't hear. He is talking about how, when a whale dies, it's called a whalefall. He says it makes this whole ecosystem on the ocean floor that lasts for decades. Years and years of animals rummaging through its bones and eating dead skin and maybe hiding inside of it. He says even though a blue whale is the largest animal on earth, and even though everyone talks about how it can fit an elephant inside its mouth, it can't manage to swallow anything bigger than a grapefruit. Doctor says that's really good to know. High Five says thank god. Whaleman loves whales so much I really think he wants to be one. I think that's really human of us, that we want to be other things. I don't think other things want to be us. I think it is only us who walk around not wanting to be us.

We want to be so many things. But we are also ourselves. We want to be so many things. But we are also ourselves. We want to be so many things. But we are also ourselves. We want to be so many things. But we are also ourselves. We want to be so many things. But we are also ourselves. We want to be so many things. But we are also ourselves. We want to be so many things. But we are also ourselves. We want to be so many things. But we are also ourselves. We want to be so many things. But we are also ourselves. We want to be so many things. But we are also ourselves. We want to be so many things. But we are also ourselves. We want to be so many things. But we are also ourselves. We want to be so many things. But we are also ourselves. We want to be so many things. But we are also ourselves.

I'd be a different person, first of all. Or I'd be a leaf, just to see what it's like to wait one whole life to fall. I'd be grass in the wind. I think it'd be nice to be a road. I think the pressure would feel good. I bet a road is asleep all the time. I'd be a fish swimming between a dead whale's bones. I'd be a mouse living in the walls of a house. I'd be the belt my father hit me with, and I'd stop myself the moment before I hit a little boy's skin. I'd hang there in the air and confuse everyone. No one would know what to do. My dad would look so confused. Sorry, too. I'd be no harm, no harm, no foul. I'd be ice that freezes everyone in place. And everyone would have to touch, like tongues to a pole. I'd have all these nerves running through my water. So everyone frozen everywhere would touch everyone frozen everywhere. No violence. Only touch, frozen like that. And still.

All girls are short except for the ones who are tall. High Five is not one of the tall ones. But she smiles really big and says high five when anyone says or does something that she thinks is awesome. For High Five, awesome is most things. She says high five when I see a deer in the woods. She says high five when we reach the top of a small rise and see a valley stretching out below. She says high five when Whaleman complains about a blister. She says high five when she tells a joke about how much she hates U2. She says high five when just before we are about to cross a road, she says that she bets we are about to cross a road. We give High Five high fives on the road. When I give High Five a high five, it's more like a regular five. It's even a low one. She holds her hand up but it barely comes to my head. So I reach my hand across to meet her raised hand. High Five.

I think most people are terrible. Actually, I think all people are terrible. When someone is terrible to you, it makes all people seem terrible. Especially when that someone is your dad, and when he seems, most of the time, mostly good. But then he does something like make you bend over and hit you because you did something that didn't seem so bad but maybe he thought it was really bad. I think that's bad. It's bad to not explain the why of things. It's bad to punish without explaining. I think that's really mean. I think people do that kind of meanness all the time. I think the world is made into what it is because of that meanness. And so I think it is a mean world. When all people have a terribleness in them, it explains more than if all people have only a goodness or only a niceness or only a kindness. Because, if all people are good or nice or kind, then the terrible things seem the most terrible. They seem like things you have to find reasons for. Things that you have to explain in your mind, over and over, because you think all people are good. But if all people are terrible, then you only have to explain the goodness. But you don't, really. You can just think it's nice, and feel fine about it, and try not to depend on it. That means I'm terrible, too. For leaving my dad alone. But that makes sense. Everyone is terrible.

If everyone is terrible, then nice things are just nice. If everyone is terrible, then nice things are just nice. If everyone is terrible, then nice things are just nice. If everyone is terrible, then nice things are just nice. If everyone is terrible, then nice things are just nice. If everyone is terrible, then nice things are just nice. If everyone is terrible, then nice things are just nice. If everyone is terrible, then nice things are just nice. If everyone is terrible, then nice things are just nice. If everyone is terrible, then nice things are just nice. If everyone is terrible, then nice things are just nice. If everyone is terrible, then nice things are just nice. If everyone is terrible, then nice things are just nice. If everyone is terrible, then nice things are just nice. If everyone is terrible, then nice things are just nice. If everyone is terrible, then nice things are just nice. If everyone is terrible, then nice things are just nice.

Doctor is Doctor because he is a doctor. Or almost is. He says med school was taking too long. He says med school wore him thin. He says he got too tired too quickly. He says everything sucked. He tells stories about watching a baby being born, and then another, and then another. He knows how to intubate and set a broken bone and create a tourniquet out of almost anything. We walk along the trail, and that could be a tourniquet, or that, or that. Anything can be a tourniquet if you bend it enough without breaking. He is almost too smart. It is like walking with someone who has been to college many times. Sometimes, he cannot stand the talking. He puts in headphones and listens to "Country Roads." When he does this, everyone still talks. Mostly I listen. Whaleman talks about whales and High Five thinks everything is awesome and I walk right behind them and try to keep up.

Whaleman says people say that no one knows why whales beach themselves. He spends miles talking about it. 1,000 whales on an island in New Zealand. 300 whales in Chile. 470 in Tasmania. He pauses for a while to think about it all. He stares up at the trees. He picks up a stick and puts it down. We are silent. I am silent and Doctor is silent and High Five is silent. Whaleman says that people say no one knows why whales beach themselves. He says it again and again. But then he says they do know why. He says there are submarine tests that mess with the whale's heads. Their big, bulby heads is what he says. He says there is so much shipping traffic. All these big boats. Red boats, orange boats, green boats. All too big for the whales to know what to do. He says the whales must be so scared. He says think about the finbacks, trying to say hello. He is gesturing wildly now. He is almost crying. They are trying to say hello but they can't. He says it loud. When he says can't his voice gets a little squeaky. He says they are trying to say hello but too many things get in the way.

Rocks jagged, boulders crooked. Learning how to live this life. One step, then another. Okay. Fine. There is time not yet had. And all the hours passed. If anything, make me less. Little leaf hanging on a branch. Suntime swirl. Nighttime nocturne. Wandering soul dream-dreaming. Miss, missing, missed. Love, loving, loved. It will be a while. Long, longing, prolonged. Today, I walked. Listened. Laughed. Cried.

Found Letter From Mother To Father

March 1st, 2001

Hey. Here's a superpower of a reminder. The stars you see are the stars I see. That's all I can think or say right now. The stars you see. Are the stars I see. When you see a star. I see the same star. It's the same. The whole weird-god-who-made-it sky. The same for you, for me. The same for both of us. It's like a blanket that covers us both.

It's chilly here at night, in the desert. They give us water to drink and when someone has a real craving for something strong, they put a lemon in it. Someone I met chews ice all day. I am writing this with a lemon in my water. Look, I know you are with the kids. So I need to say it: thank you. Thank you for that. I put a smaller letter inside this one. It's for the two of them. It says what I told you. About the stars being the same. About all of us looking together.

What can I say? It is hard here. It's really fucking hard. Everyone has their stories. I hear them each day. We sit in a circle and everyone shares. They are hard stories. They are stories of people failing. Failing themselves or failing others.

I close my eyes and I am back there. I am sitting in a dark room that does not have the power of dreams. It's really real, this room. And one woman is telling a story. She's leaving her baby in the car while she goes into a bar, and when she comes back outside, drunk and lonely and teetering, her car's window is slammed into shards and someone she doesn't even know was holding her baby. God, imagine. Imagine! There's glass on the ground. And she talks about that. She talks about staring at the shattered glass, and she talks about how it glittered in the moonlight, and she talks about not wanting to look up, to see this man holding her baby that she had left alone for hours. And she says, in that nightmare room, that this was when she knew, and we all nod, because, I think, we all know what it is like to know. To know something like that. To know it for certain.

But before you judge her, can I say I felt for her? Do I sound terrible, feeling for her? They have words like neglect to describe an action like that. They can make that word into a crime. They have phrases like she didn't love her child, how could a mother not love her child, she shouldn't be a mother, take her baby away, lock her up, a special place in hell, she deserves it, how could she, how could she, how could she. But no one talks about how we each run away at some point. Some people run away every day. They come back, usually always on time. No one talks about that. What makes someone run, and how human it is.

I remember that poem I wrote:

>How can you chase yourself
>If you are yourself? It must be like
>the sea, never knowing if you are
>touching the land or pulling away.

I am trying to write again. Little short things. I feel like Emily Dickinson. I can't finish a thought. It is all blank space. Incompletion.

Who am I—

Dare I say—

I don't know—

Do you understand—

Maybe you don't. Treat the kids well. Look up together at the stars.

They'll get it. I am trying to get better for them. I am trying not to leave anyone in the car. I am trying not to leave. I am trying! But I want you to know: I feel it. I feel that dark part inside of me. I can't say I don't. And when you meet yourself for the first time, and when you see it there, lingering dark matter at the heart of you, and when you understand it there in others—tell me, how can you forget it? And should you forget it at all? They say getting better has to begin with yourself here. But that seems hard. That seems really hard.

Yours...

Brother Keene

Patti opened the fence and let the dogs out. Some turned down the road and sprinted for what seemed like forever, until they diminished into little specks approaching a horizon. The rest bounded across the asphalt and into a field on the road's other side. Soon, they were just rustles in the tall grass.

Will they come back, I said.

They'll come back, Patti said. If not—

She shrugged.

The melted sun diluted the sky. I counted three dogs, then just two, then four. *O Peace*, Merton wrote, *bless this mad place*. Was this peace? A sun above the world, the dogs running free, a brother gone missing, bread almost risen? It seemed more like peace mixed with madness, a little touch of light to illuminate the dark. I had wanted once, out of curiosity, not sure how badly, to leave this world, and live a little above it. Now I was in the world and it felt so very different and so very much the same.

Are you happy where you are, I said.

Happy isn't the right word for it, Patti said.

We both watched the dogs. They were hurling their bodies at each other now, like atoms let loose in some experiment, bumping and playing and separating and bumping again. Their tongues seemed to grow larger each second, until they hung like willow branches out of the trucks of their long necks.

It's like, she said, it's like I know there could be something better. I guess I know that. Maybe I don't. But sure. Yes. Yes I do. There could be something better. But then you spend enough days in the same place with the same things. You know? You wake up and wake the dogs and have your cigarette. It's fine. You learn to like it. I guess that's love, maybe. Learning to like something. I guess that is love.

Maybe, I said.

And you know, she said, then that something better or someplace better? Well, it just becomes what it is. *Some* thing. *Some* place. Not this one. No. It's not as real as *this* place. With the dogs and the road and the morning. It's fine, you know? It's fine.

It is fine, I said. It's very fine.

Five dogs in the distance, then two disappearing into the grass. A math problem. The answer? Three dogs in the distance.

Once, I said, I was talking with the Abbot at the monastery. And he said that maybe committing to something is God. Like, God is in the action. We were talking about God.

As monks do, Patti said.

As we do, yes. Just talk about God. And so he said maybe committing to something is God. And I said well what about people who commit to all sorts of odd things. There are people out there committing to excess, greed, all that bad stuff. I think I was thinking about my mother. He looked at me funny. Like, he really squinted at me. He said I was always worrying about other people. Other people's problems. Their desires. And not just worrying about them. You're always imposing judgment, he said. He said that. You don't know the nature of their commitments, he said. You hardly know your own.

Ouch, Patti said.

Yeah, I said. And I remember sitting there and thinking to myself: if I don't know the nature of my own commitments, how could I claim to know myself? Let alone God?

Your mother, she said. Why were you thinking about her?

She drank and then she left, I said. When I was a kid. I was angry at her for a long time.

Are you angry now?

No, I said. No I'm not. I think of her walking along the beach. I think of her like this wild machine of light. Something that takes light in and grows and grows and grows. I think of her in the morning, becoming who she is. There's no anger anymore.

What changed?

I thought of my friend, then, how he said *I'm sorry*, over and over again.

I realized, I said, how hard it is, sometimes, to be alive.

Maybe all the time, Patti said.

The dogs came wandering back. Oslo brought up the rear, tongue drooling out the side of his mouth, looking like a skinny and haggard champion.

Inside, I preheated the oven and took the towel off the loaf. The dough had risen. It was light, flecked with dry bits. I wasn't always like this. Sometimes, as a kid, I didn't know what patience was. I was older and Billy was young. He had his questions. Mom this, Dad that. He wanted to know why. Why anything, why everything. I said no often. I slammed the door. I can never go back.

The heat from the oven made the dough rise more. It pushed against itself, all this air trying to escape. It crusted up almost everywhere, but not in the center, where the slim arc I had etched into the top broke and bent open. A baked loaf of bread is like something that almost exploded, but didn't. It is frozen in the act of almost blowing itself apart. I looked at it inside the oven. I wondered if it was a sign. I wanted to learn something about this life. That maybe we are like that, too. But the oven was a door, and I could open it. So I did. I wrapped a towel around my hand and lifted the pan out of the oven. I set it on the stove to cool.

The loaf crackled, all that steam trying to escape. I put my ear to it. I put my ear closer.

Crackle, it said.

Pop, I said.

Crackle, it said.

Who's there, I said.

My voice was a whisper. I was talking to the loaf of bread. It sounded like static on the other end. Divine static. The stuff of life. What you would hear if you picked up a phone in heaven, right before you dialed down to earth. I held my ear closer. It was like holding a tin can on the other side of a magic door to a room of the past, where people were talking.

I don't want to, my mom said.

Then don't, my dad said. If you don't want to, don't. It's simple.

It's a chokehold, this life, my mom said. You wouldn't understand.

Why does anyone say that? Does anyone who says that even try to make someone understand?

It's a longer life than I imagined. I need to make it mine.

But it's ours, now, my dad said. It's too late for that. Look at what we have. Look at who.

No one asks a tree if it's okay with the fence built around it.

But this isn't a poem, my dad said. This is our life.

It's mine, too.

Ours.

I need to make it mine.

Hello, I said. Dad? Mom?

I looked up and I was in a kitchen and holding a loaf of bread to my ear and Patti was staring at me.

Sorry, I said. I think it's time to go.

Let me drive you somewhere, she said.

I unfolded the gas station map and showed her the yellow line.

Can you show me where we are, I said.

Patti pointed a finger at a spot almost exactly halfway between where the line began and where it ended. I met her finger and moved mine further down along the line, to the next town with a name. She did not ask about the map. I think she understood.

Can you drive me here?

I can drive you there.

She offered me some of her ex-husband's clothes, rolled up and ready to be stuffed in my bag. I stuffed them in my bag. When we got in the car, Oslo bounded up into the front and through the space between the seats until he was wedged, once again, in the back. It happened so fast that, if I wasn't looking, I wouldn't have known he was there. And soon we were driving down the road where the dogs had once run. We drove silently, not talking, only a CD playing on low, one I didn't know, but one that Patti would occasionally mouth along to. *Are you alright*, one song went. *Are you alright. Are you alright.*

Maybe God was at work, I thought. And then immediately I felt a little bit of shame at such a cliché. But here I was, still unable to drive, being driven—once again—by someone else. I had gotten so far on the kindness of others. Was that God? Or someone else? It certainly wasn't me.

In high school, I took and failed the driving test three times. Each time, I barely made it out of the lot where it all started. I'd press the pedal gently and set the thing in motion. And then I'd lock up. All of a sudden, the car felt like what it was, what I had to tell myself it wasn't: so big, too big. I'd start whispering at the wheel. *I can control you I can control you I can control you.* But I couldn't. The wheel felt too small for such a beast. I felt too tiny in the seat. Each time, before the first turn, I'd stop and rest my forehead in my hands. *I can't I can't I can't.* That's what I'd say. And it's true. I couldn't.

My friends would drive me everywhere. To the movies. To the diner after the movies. Sometimes home from school. It got to be a joke. All the gas money I'd owe when we were older, and rich, and still friends. Older, not rich, and not friends, I thought that maybe all of that—the driving, the joking, the doing it all over again—was kindness we never could admit as such. There always had to be a cost. A payment to be delivered at a future date. We couldn't admit that it was fine. That people didn't have to know how to drive. That friends could act like, well, friends. That I could accept that. And then I got older and everything felt already a little too late. Time unstretches itself from its long distance. Maybe that's God. Maybe God is the landlord asking for the rent. In the car with Patti, I had either escaped God's grasp or escaped back into it, where there was kindness once more, and the long road driven in mostly silence, and what we do for others without judgment. Maybe you have to leave the world to find it.

You know, Patti said.

You know, I said, I know you're about to talk when you say you know.

You know, she said, I was wrong. I do get lonely still. I haven't really figured it out.

I don't think you said you had.

Yeah, well. Haven't.

She put one hand to her heart while she drove.

Scout's honor, she said.

Monk's honor, I said.

She looked straight ahead. She could have fallen asleep. The road was so straight and so long. She could have fallen asleep and nothing bad would have happened.

It's just, she said. I haven't gotten used to it. To being alone. I haven't gotten used to the silence, and the way there is no one there when I wake up and want someone there, and how those dogs run away and how they look like they'll never come back and my god, who is going to eat all the food in the fridge, there's jam that's five years old. And then the dogs come back and I feel like I don't deserve it. I haven't gotten used to that. To feeling like I don't deserve something. Even the big sadness I feel when I look around at the empty room and my grandma's couch and say well I guess this is my life and then the big softness in my heart when a dog pops his head into the room and then fills it with his whole body. I don't know what I did. Everyone is saying do this. Do that. All this talk. Make your life. I've done so much. I've done enough to make a life. This is my life. Cooking food for one and slopping enough dog food in enough bowls to feed a dozen.

She turned her head quickly to look at me and then resumed her stare down the one long road.

What would God say, she said.

Which God, I said. Some days it seems like there's a bunch.

I don't know. Pick one.

I think God would say it's true you've done enough. I think God would have a real sympathy for you. Something profound and big. I think he would apologize, even. I think he'd say he's sorry. And that the world is messy and filled with people, and people are messy, and they do messy things. And I think, maybe, he'd say something a little stupid at first. Something dumb. Like, you can make the best of this.

Yeah, that's fucking stupid. I'd punch him.

Yes, I said. He'd deserve it. And he'd get all flustered I think, because he could see that. He could see his stupidity there. And he'd take it back. Maybe he'd stammer a bit and bumble something stupid again and then take that back, too. And then he'd get real quiet, and you'd think he'd say something really beautiful this time, on his tenth try, but all he'd say is I don't know.

I don't know, Patti said.

Yeah, I don't know, I said. You've got to imagine it, too. Big beard and everything. Huge face, probably. Blushing a bit. Stammering. You have to imagine that. Mostly the huge face. Like, a really huge face.

You know, Patti said, I think I'd like that. If God came down and walked through my door and blushed. God, I'd love that. I'd say God, I love you, you lunatic. Giving your big, elaborate responses to this big mess of a world. And then just blushing and saying I don't know. I think I'd love that. I'd laugh so hard. I'd laugh in his face. I bet he would laugh, too.

You'd laugh?

I'd laugh so fucking hard. You have no idea.

Patti blinked fast forty-three times and then banged her hand against the wheel and then her forehead and when she came up her eyes were filled with tears and she was laughing.

I don't know, she said.

She started laughing more, laughing louder. Soon, the whole car was filled with laughter. I was laughing, too. My eyes were welling up, little bits of water around the tops of my cheeks. I don't know, we kept saying, in between laughs that came out of us like burps, these guttural, soulful things we couldn't control. I don't know, I don't know, I don't know. We were laughing so hard. The windows were down and Patti's hair was in her eyes and her tears were bits of ocean spray slipping off her cheek and Oslo in the back was looking at us curiously and maybe even with something approaching a smile, his tongue bouncing up and down outside the side of his mouth. I don't know, we kept saying, laughing as we said it.

After a while, we rolled to a stop. We were on the other side of the state line, parked at a gas station. There was a small store attached to it: George's Market. Patti opened the window, lit a cigarette.

Here you are, she said. The next town on the yellow line.

This is as far as I go, she said.

This is where I go, I said.

And then:

Thank you, I said.

Patti shrugged, looked out the window, ashed her cigarette.

It's been, she said.

And then she shrugged again, put the cigarette in her mouth.

I know, I said. Well—

You don't, she said.

I've never really said goodbye before, I said. I've always just, well, kind of left.

I guess if you say goodbye, Patti said, then it means you can't come back. Sometimes it helps to leave the door open.

And that was that. I shouldered my bag and headed southeast, destined to follow the yellow line. I only made it a few steps when I heard a sound. Like the patter of a little mouse, growing larger and louder. I turned and there was Oslo. Tongue out.

Really fucking skinny. He was all bone, no skin.

You know, Patti said.

She was yelling. Her head out the window of the car. Just like when I met her. Streaks of orange rust along the side of the vehicle. Streaks of orange in her hair. The orange ember of her cigarette.

I thought he might do that, she said. There's food for him in your bag.

Food is good, I said. He needs it.

I was yelling, too. We were already so far apart. How did life happen like that? And why?

She began to turn the car around and I turned before I could watch her drive away. But I heard it: the low, gurgling rumble of the engine. The tires on the road. Everything getting faster as everything pulled apart. And soon it was just me and the dog, somewhere in Pennsylvania.

What to do then but walk? Oslo had no leash. He simply trotted along beside me and then bounded away and then came back and bounded away again. He was a beating heart with legs—so full of anxiety and goodwill and longing and desire and speed. The kind of animal that would be endless, if things never had to come to an end. It's funny, the heart. It just beats. It beats and beats and beats. And then it doesn't. It has nothing to say. It can't speak at all. It can't make a word out of its ventricle, a tongue in the valve. And yet, it matters what it does. It is the only thing that matters. It allows. It does not speak, but it speaks. It has no voice, no brain, no ears, but it sounds, it thinks, it hears. We know how it works but don't know how. And when that happens, you also don't know why. And it's the why that boggles the mind. It's the why that drives men to God, that throws a single body off a bridge into the water below. It's the why, and the way the why dangles there, ever unanswerable at a certain point. Why is life hard, I wondered. Because you only know so much.

The road was good for such wondering.

Hello, the road said.

Hi, I said.

Maybe the path is just a path of thought.

Are you saying that you are not real, road?

Ouch, the road said.

What happened?

The car, the road said. It just ran over me.

Oh, I said. Oh, no.

Ouch, the road said. Not again!

Oslo clung to my leg and the world reminded both of us that the world was, in fact, a world: full of the beating hearts of so many people doing so many things. I imagined the world before, before what drove me to despair: the buildings, and the people inside of them, and the money they made from trying to build bigger buildings. It must have been full of a few people, that world before. And their dogs. And the tamped-down paths through the grass of the people who had come before. There must have been such stillness. A great acknowledgment of distance. Or maybe an absolute ignorance. But there must have been the intimacy of people together in close spaces, understanding that the world was a thing too big and wide to know. And so, they must have huddled close with those they were close with. They must have felt a powerful silence that sat with them. I bet they respected that silence. It must have been impossible to ignore, the way a car ignores the silence it drives through by driving through it, the way a party ignores the silence at the heart of it by playing music.

I, too, tried to ignore the silence. I said good dog to Oslo whenever I could.

I said what was life like, Oslo, racing around that track?

I said are you happy now? I said are you afraid? I said do you think of everything in between?

Oslo didn't respond. Sometimes he looked up at me in the way that dogs do, with his head turned a little bit backward and a little bit sideways, his tongue filling the space between the two of us. When he did such a thing, I felt better to be in his world than he probably did to be in mine.

I thought of my dad, then, talking to someone who never answered. At the next gas station, some few hours down the road, I fed coins into the pay phone just outside the bathroom. I was surprised that it was even there, and that it worked. He answered after just one ring.

Hello, he said.

His voice wavered with a tight, vibrating anxiety. It sounded unlike the voice I grew up with, which was like when you shift all the music in a car until it is playing out of the speakers in the front two seats. It was always *there*, his voice was. Now, it sounded like it had shifted to the rear.

I realized then that he must have thought I was someone with information about Billy. He must have seen some odd number and thought I was calling with news.

Hey Dad.

There was a pause, and in that pause I could hear a shallow breath, and then an attempt at a deeper one.

Oh. It's you.

It's me, Dad.

Sorry, I thought—

It's okay. I know. I'm sorry.

Why are you calling, he said.

I wanted to see how you were. I was thinking of you.

You were thinking of me, he said. How do you think I am?

I don't know, Dad. That's why I'm calling.

I'm fine, he said. I'm fine.

A car pulled in. Someone got out, went inside. Someone else got out and threw the biggest cup of soda into the smallest trash can. Oslo sniffed at the bottom of the bathroom door.

I know you're not fine, I said. It's okay. I wouldn't be fine.

And how would you know?

Because I'm not fine, either. How could either of us be fine? How could anyone?

I don't know, he said. You're just—you're gone, too.

I'm not gone, Dad.

You're not here.

Am I supposed to be?

I felt the heat of his sigh through the phone. I had never heard my dad come close to crying. I closed my eyes and saw his eyes widening and then blinking once and then blinking again, blinking blinking blinking the tears away. I could see the water pool over the whites of eyes, even though I had never seen water pool over the whites of his eyes. I remembered how I had cried, hearing their voices in the other room. The loneliness of waiting for them to remember me. The way, blinking into the dark, tears don't obscure anything. The way it was just dark and more dark.

What ailed thee, O brother, that thou fleddest, I said, not realizing I had said it until it left my mouth.

Is that a Bible verse?

No, not really. Well, sort of. It's an off-brand one.

He laughed, almost. And then a long pause. The person who had entered the station came out with a fistful of cash, and began to pump gas. The other person put their feet up on the dashboard of the passenger seat, shoes off, hat over their eyes.

Dad, I said, do you remember the road trips? How you'd stick a twenty in my hand at the gas station?

You'd come back with Necco Wafers, he said.

I don't know why I liked them, I said. Sometimes they were so stale. And sometimes in the dark I couldn't figure out which was chocolate or licorice or grape.

You just gave all the dark ones to me.

Yeah, I said. I did.

I loved licorice, he said.

I know.

The pump clicked. The car door opened. The man got inside, slapped the hat off the other person's head. Laughter I couldn't hear.

Can you tell me, my Dad said, about forgiveness?

I don't know much about it, Dad. I haven't had to forgive much.

Not me? Not your mom?

Dad, I said, what can I say? People leave.

I know, he said. I know they do.

Is there something—

I just. It's my fault.

You don't know that.

I was hard on him when you were gone.

You were hard always, I said. But it's you. You were always you.

No, he said. You don't understand. I—

What are you trying to say?

I don't know, he said.

Everything outside of the phone felt more like a dream. The long road and the sun above it. It was hard to believe that there was a world other than the sound of my voice, and then the sound of my father's.

I just want to know about forgiveness, he said.

Sometimes, I said, forgiveness just means going on with your life.

And doing it better, I guess. Better than before.

I'd rather just not have done before. Who can I apologize to now? It's the wrong that I remember. I don't think of the better.

Have you forgiven Mom, I said.

No.

Well. Maybe you should.

How?

I think you just do it, Dad.

And if Billy never comes home?

He was crying, then. I could hear it in the caught breath. It was like he was trying to swallow his soul back into his body.

Dad, I said, this is our life.

It's just not how I pictured it.

What is, Dad? Seriously, what is?

Do you pray, he said. Up there, wherever you are?

Yes, Dad. We pray all day.

Can you pray for us?

I do, I said. I will.

I hung up the phone. I didn't know what to do. I thought of those long road trips with him. I thought of one years ago, road tripping with Dad while Mom stayed home with Billy. The way he put the money in my hand. I returned with Necco Wafers, a Diet Coke, the rest of the cash on pump three.

How had it come so far, so fast? Billy's legs—pale, wiry, young—ran across my mind. We weren't that broken. We were just a little bit broken. What isn't? Now, we were pieces.

That road trip, my dad got a call from Mom while in the car. He began to yell. Something about money. Something about alcohol. Something about having to call someone again.

And the car, he said. And the car, and the car, and the car.

Where is it, he said.

It was dark and he had one hand on the wheel but his whole soul and all of its anger was in the phone. His eyes stared through the windshield into the fever dream of his life. When he hung up, he looked like a lamp caught in the process of becoming dark. He whispered about Mom.

Get your ass in order, he said.

I was young, not even a teenager. I thought of her reading to me in bed. How could anyone be wrong at any time? To hear him whisper was to hear pain.

Shut up, Dad, I said.

I said it as softly as I could. And he did. I don't know if it was because of me. Or just because. I watched the yellow windows of houses in the distance, far off the highway, and wondered about what happened inside of them.

Outside the gas station, I picked up the phone I had just hung up, and I slammed it into the receiver. I picked it up and slammed it again. One more time for good measure. Oslo, once gathered at my feet, became a streak of faded color that said once, there was a dog standing here. I looked into the distance. He had sprinted away at the sound of the noise.

Fuck, I said.

I began to walk. I walked the straight line I had seen him run, along the side of the road that cut through Pennsylvania. I fumed. I raged. I wept, thinking of how this journey had started in search of one living being and had just become a journey in search of two.

Oslo, I said.

I whispered it and then said it again as one strong, stubborn word. And then I screamed it. And then I whispered it again. Over and over.

Oslo. Oslo. Oslo.

Perhaps it is best, I thought, for everyone to retreat to a monastery of their own making. To hillsides and hilltops. Places where the sun is not in competition with anything else, where there is only the kind of blue the sky gets when you can see all of it, and clouds feel like the breath of the million angels who live inside of that blue-painted room. Perhaps there is nothing for us out here, in this place we have already ruined. Dogs run at the sound of human-made things. People run at the sound of other people. What pattern have we created on this earth that is not a pattern of harm? Perhaps the only way to love anything is to let it go, knowing, too, that if you don't it will go on its own because of you.

I walked for hours, until I couldn't walk anymore. The sun, as it set, cast a purple glow over the road's white line. And then it set, and there was nothing but the distant light of a car moving toward me. The light grew wider and brighter—a star on the horizon shooting itself across the flat land. I almost wished upon it, but then it grew so wide and so bright that I had to turn my head away. And with a rush and a roar, the light was gone, and the darkness resumed.

In my first memory of my mother, we are sitting outside in the night's pitch black, on my first vacation. There is water nearby, and the sound of it is this gentle, unending thing. It comes and comes and comes. It never goes. It is endless. We aren't talking. We are just sitting there. I hold my knees to my chest, and my mom is next to me, staring up between the trees at the star-speckled sky above. Then, I feel her hand on my knee. My mom's hand. My knee. I feel it so tight I almost scream. She yells. Her hand lifts and points toward the sky. A shooting star. That's what she says. She says it once very quietly, as if she forgets I am around. But then she says it again, rushed, loud, with more urgency. She wants to include me. She wants me to find it. I follow her finger as it trails behind the star. I look up and up. I try to see what she saw, but I can't. And soon, the star falls behind the trees, and, I imagine, all the way out of the sky. I don't know why anyone wishes on such a thing. It always, without fail, goes away.

In the distance shone a neon halo. As I walked, the halo took the form of a sign. And the sign took the form of letters. VACANCY, it said. I was about to walk in, pay for a room with fifty of the few hundred dollars I still had, until I saw a soft light glowing on the motel's other side, like someone had pitched a tent and lit a lantern inside of it. I walked toward it. The light stayed small. Warm. Someone was inside with the light, throwing their shadow outward. And someone else was, too. There were two shadows. They were talking to each other.

Hey pup, one shadow said.

The other shadow did not respond.

Oslo, I said, and both shadows became alive.

In front of me sat someone just like me—young, concerned, slightly wild. And Olso, too, head turned sideways at my hand, which still held a can of food. It seemed he doubted my hand but trusted the food. I put it on the ground, and Oslo began to eat.

The other shadow did not get up. He was sitting down. The neon of the motel's sign reflected off of the metal frame upon which he sat. His hands rested on two wheels.

Hi, I said. I'm looking for that dog.

Hi, he said. I'm rolling across the country.

Billy Keene

They used to ask me why I am here. Now they do not. I would never say. I think it made them uncomfortable. It made them sad. Skinny boy in the woods. They must think I'm odd. At night, I sleep in the same tent as Doctor, and he keeps humming the same songs. I ask them why they are here. Does anyone need a reason, Whaleman says. Why wouldn't I be, High Five says. Doctor does not answer at first. It seems that Whaleman and High Five know. They don't pester. They don't pry. After one long silence on top of a mountain, Doctor looks at the trail below. He says he was working the ER on the day of a shooting. He says they wheeled in one person, bloody and terrified, and everyone began to help. Everyone rushed, Doctor says. In their rushing, they didn't see the others. One after another after another. All the same kind of bloody, some worse. Some died, Doctor says, just inside. By the reception desk. In front of people filling out forms for their husbands having heart attacks. He says he tried to help who he could. Anything could become a tourniquet if you need a tourniquet bad enough. But the need, he says, the need was too great. There was too much need and not enough help. People died, he says. And the way he says it, there's a bit of anger and a bit of something else. I guess it's what I would call nofuckingclue. When the world is too much. When there are no words. That's what I feel, hearing Doctor speak. For a long time, there's silence. Then he begins to hum a song. We hum along.

I liked to run because I didn't have to have a reason. I could just say I liked to run, and people would understand. No one would say run where? Or run away? No one would ask me to explain. I could go for a run and be alone and feel better than any other time that day. People call that free. I could be free, if that's what I called free. But each time I went for a run, I also had to be done with it, sometime, somewhere. And then, I'd be back in the world. It was a world where first Mom left, then my brother, and where even Dad would come home late. I played the piano my mom left. I made up names on the internet. I did it all in the space that people left me with. I became a different person, trying to be myself in a world I didn't like. I don't know how to share that with anyone.

The Greenland Shark is the oldest shark in the world, Whaleman says. In fact, he says, it's the oldest living vertebrae. He says the Greenland Shark can live up to 500 years. He says it lives so deep, in the coldest depths of the ocean, where it is so dark, darker than anything we think of as dark. He says its skin is poisonous because it has this super chemical inside of it that keeps it warm. There's a tiny parasite that also lives that deep in the ocean, Whaleman says. He says the parasite attaches itself to the shark's eyes, and slowly degenerates it. Eventually, at some point in its 500-year life, the shark goes blind. But it is so dark underwater that it doesn't really matter.

Trees have names. I don't know them. Everything called something, most life going by unknown, unaware. One day, maybe? Doubtful. Instead, time to walk. Heel, mid foot, toe. Blister, hangnail, ingrown pain. A journey of how many miles? Begins with what? Light on leaves. Flower power. Tired, but still—think that it all goes on. With. Without. Forever. Until. Even. If. When. Never. Still. No words repeated except for all. Why leave anything? Nothing else does.

We eat our ramen bombs on these rocks overlooking a valley. The rocks are named after a town we are nowhere near. We go to bed before twilight, and watch the sunset as dessert. Whaleman points to these lights in the distance. See those, he says. See how they are arranged in a perfect square. We each nod. That's a prison, he says. High Five makes a sad face. No high fives for that, she says. Definitely not, Doctor says. I don't say anything. I can only think if there are windows there, and, if there are, if the people down there can see us up here, looking down at them. What, High Five says. I have to speak. I say nothing. I say I am just embarrassed at a phrase I came up with in my head. I say the phrase was look down at them. And then I point at the prison. We are looking at the prison. Thinking the same things. I am always thinking, I think. I bet, down there, so many people are. I want to write a letter and throw it to them. But it is too far and I don't want anyone to get hurt. You have a new name, Doctor says. It is Wondering. Wondering, I say out loud, trying it on for size. Wondering, we all say.

When my brother left, Dad got mad, and we were all alone. His anger was everywhere. It was in the couch and in our dinner and on the TV and in the telephone's ring and in his words, since I had grown out of his belt. Sometimes, sitting next to him, he grabbed my leg just above the knee and squeezed it until both our eyes teared up, and then he let it go. It was like he had just woken from a trance. He smiled. I smiled, too, and we watched the sports on the screen. The house was not big or small. It was the size of a house. I waited enough time for him to think I wasn't going upstairs because of him, and then I went upstairs. Those were the years I dreamed I was so small I could fit under the cracks of doors. I sometimes fell from my bed while dreaming those dreams. I fell from my bed often. My brother sometimes caught me, and I never thanked him. But he was gone, then, so I hit the floor and then woke up.

Someone going the other way warns us about a rattlesnake. Rattlesnake, he says, about 200 yards up the trail, right side. So we all go to the left and walk single file. I know how far 200 yards is. I don't say it, but I know. A rattlesnake is a rattlesnake. We stay on the left side for a long time. We pass 200 yards. We pass a quarter mile. We walk a mile without talking, each of us looking straight to our right, picking our feet high off the ground. I think: if it was a joke, it was a cruel one, but also funny. We stay on the left side of the trail for what seems like forever. Maybe it is good practice, to always be wary. High Five says okay, it has been 200 yards. It has been an hour. We laugh. We let out one big together-sigh. High Five says high five for the person to go to the right side. Doctor begins to walk that way. He begins for a long time. It takes him forever. I think we are always scared of some things, and sometimes we are really scared of them.

I am always scared and it's okay. I am always scared and it's fine. I am always scared and it's terrifying. I am always scared and it's beautiful. I am always scared and it's like flying. I am always scared and it's a big huge hole in my chest. I am always scared and it's how I know I am alive. I am always scared and it's perfect. I am always scared and it's depressing. I am always scared and it's one big stupid joke. I am always scared and it's weird. I am always scared and it's really, really weird. I am always scared and it's for the dumbest reasons. I am always scared and it's the most important thing in the world. I am always scared and it's who I am. I am always scared and it's what makes me me. I am always scared and it's a lie. I am always scared and it's the goddamn honest truth. I am always scared and it's brutal. I am always scared and it's scary. I am always scared and it's clipping my wings. I am always scared and it's not like flying anymore. I am always scared and it's a growth as big as me on the side of my body. I am always scared and it's okay.

We pass an orange around and sit on a picnic table in a clearing. A couple walks up to us. Hi, one says. We are Stick and Poke. I am Stick and this is Poke. Stick waves, then Poke. High five, High Five says, and gives them a high five. Also, she says, that's my name. High Five. And this is Doctor, Whaleman, and Wondering. A good gang, Poke says. Really great, Stick says. They tell us they live on the trail, giving stick and poke tattoos. Getting a few bucks here and there. They walk north to Maine and then back south to Georgia and then back north to Maine. Do you want one, they say. Doctor makes a face, says no. I just look away. Whaleman seems intrigued. High Five holds out her hands. Can you do High Five on my knuckles she says. Stick grins. Poke grins. Of course, they say. They take out hand sanitizer and a needle. They take out a little container of ink. It takes a little while but High Five smiles the whole time. When they are done, she pretends she is a boxer. Come and fight me, Whaleman, she says. He stands up and she makes her fists. You think you want to fight, she says, but then you see this, and boom! High Five!

At camp that night, they turn to me and say: we think we know you ran away. It's okay. Your secret is safe with us. I give them each a little smile. High Five keeps looking at her fingers. For as long as it takes, Doctor says. It takes strength to be on your own, he says. Whaleman looks up at the fading light. He talks about how whales, once separated from their pods, will journey for their entire lives just to find their family again. He talks about the ocean, and how big it is, and how scary that must be, to move through such a vast and dark thing to find the smallest needle in the largest haystack. I guess we are like that, he says, except we can also make our own family. Doctor looks at me. When I saw those people that day, he says, I didn't have to imagine the violence. I could just see the damage. He says: I think life is like that, all this damage, and everyone walking around with it. I feel like crying, but I don't. I am always wondering. I want to ask: why the damage? But I don't. I think I know the answer. The answer is that there is no answer.

Found Letter From Mother To Father

June 5th, 2006

I know you're upset. Though, knowing you, you might not say you are. I get it. I understand.

Here, one more time. For the kicks, right? I am closing my eyes, and you are planning a whole love-spectacle for the night I get home from rehab. You get someone to watch the kids, and you make a reservation at that place we always have walked by but never have gone to. The one tucked away from the street, the door covered in flowers. Where, when we walk by it, you peek between the blooming things to see inside. And where I ooh and ahh outside of it while you do the peeking. That night, I say I want to stay home. And you say it's fine, that we can go another time. I think I know you're a little sad about it, but you hide it well. God, you always do. And—I'm still closing my eyes—a week later, we walk past that restaurant. And it's demolished. It's an ashen ghost of once-there-were-flowers. And now I know that you're upset. Your face does that thing where your jaw looks like the coast of Maine. But you still grimace a smile.

Look, I understand. I'd be upset, too.

I think the world makes it seem like leaving is no hard thing. Sometimes, I imagine myself put on trial. I am guilty on all counts: Guilty for being a mom. Guilty for bearing children. Guilty for drinking. Guilty for drinking too much. Guilty for that time I left our car so far out of town that you had to drive to get it, and get the me that was in it. And then you had to leave the car you drove there, and wake up early to take a cab to get it the next day. Yes, guilty for all of that. I want you to know: I feel the necessary amount of guilt for all of that. Believe me, I do. Or don't believe me. I still do.

I want to tell you that I think of my leaving as something vital to me. As vital to me as having children. As vital to me as my life. That's what vital means. Vita. Vitalis. Life.

You were no easy company. Your silence. Your anger. The way I couldn't guess it at all. And how wrong I felt, for not being able to know this person I loved. That felt awful. I felt like I had no magic in me, trying to know you and not being able to. Well, look. I don't want to hurt anymore. So, I have to leave. I have left. I do not feel guilty when I say that I left for me. I feel guilty for so much, but not for that. So much is not for me. So much of us, of what we became. So much of this world. So much of the way we started to move through it. We lost touch, vital thing touch is—of ourselves and of each other. It's a superpower, that touch. We lost it.

I don't mean to send you this letter to make you upset. I just want you to understand, even if that understanding is hard, or painful, or takes one or five or twenty years. I loved you. I do not anymore. I love our children. But loving them while being with you made me not love myself. And what love can I give if I have none for me? What can I do with a self that is bone dry, pitiful? The answer is nothing.

I hope it is enough of a testament to my life that I helped you bring our children into the world. Do you remember that? Please say yes. Oh, your hair grayed within a month of it happening, but you held him so close that month. I couldn't pull him away to nurse. And now, well, I can't pull them toward me at all. I will mother them from afar. I only ask, if you are still reading this, that you don't raise them to resent me. Let them love me or not on their own terms, in their own time. I have faith big and weird and who-knows-what of this life that they will or won't. And I'm okay with that. I am trying to be okay with that.

There were days of joy with you. Please know that. That you spent three hours trying to climb a tree. I don't know why you kept trying. But let me say: it was special to watch you try. Do you understand that? It was special to watch you try. You let me watch you try. Any time you did, there was, for me, a softness. I loved when you let us be ourselves. I know we are not our worst selves in this life, but you were your worst self for so long. If I wish anything for you for the rest of your life, it is that softness, and what good you might make of it.

Brother Keene

His name was Evan. He had been rolling himself across the country in search of alternatives to capitalism. He acknowledged that this was hard. He said, basically, that he hadn't found any. His wheelchair was outfitted like an SUV in one of those outdoorsy commercials—like where a car suddenly turns off the highway and begins to climb a gravel road up a mountain and then turns off that gravel road and ascends a cliff face somewhere in Yosemite. Basically, any place on Evan's wheelchair that could have a pack tied on it had a pack tied on it. There was canvas everywhere, and with a quick backward flick of his arm, he could grab a strap that pulled a makeshift roof over his head.

Ta-da, he said.

Wow, I said.

Don't fuck with me, he said.

Who would, I said.

He was young, somewhere, it seemed, in his twenties, but the country had weathered his face into this bearded thing pocked with hollows, which made him look both foolish and wise, like Job from the Old Testament, if Job didn't let himself get so fucked over by God and everyone else. He carried a journal. He wrote poems while he rested. I wanted to read one, almost immediately upon meeting him, but he didn't offer at first.

That first night, Evan pulled a tarp from one of his seven hundred canvas bags. I spread it out for Oslo and me. We moved for hours the next morning. I offered to push him, but he said he liked the slow burn in his arms that came from rolling his wheels over and over again. He liked the repetitive motion.

All this gadgetry, I said, and no motor?

My heart is the motor of my life, Evan said.

I did a small bow of my head, and we continued moving. When Oslo got tired, Oslo sat in Evan's lap, like a weary sea captain staring out across the great expanse of asphalt.

Evan told me that he used to be a poet in Los Angeles. He told me about the city's underworld of poetry, which was maybe just the regular world of poetry. There were these parties he'd go to, invite only, word-of-mouth alone. Once there, ignored because no one knew how to talk to him without talking about his disability, he'd resign himself to a cigarette outside, where he'd overhear all the talk about who was publishing who and why. He'd smoke while sitting next to a National Book Award finalist who didn't even look at him, and then later hear them misquote someone they said they loved. They misquoted them so passionately, Evan said. A passion so bright it ashamed each star in the sky. And then, Evan said, you'd be smoking next to someone talking shit about someone who you later saw was at the party, and then, later, you'd be smoking a cigarette next to that person while they talked shit about someone else.

Funny, I said, I thought poets were supposed to be kind.

Poets make great improvisers, Evan said, sort of quoting Marx.

And you, he said, you are moving across this land, too? Why?

Well, I said, I don't know how to put it any other way.

Than what?

I was a monk, I said. And then my brother ran away. And now I'm looking for my brother.

Mercy, he said.

Mercy?

Mercy. I've been thinking lately that almost every decision has something to do with mercy.

Yeah?

The chair will do that for you. I don't think I'm at the mercy of others, but I do think I am calibrated to pay more attention to the fact of whether or not it is offered.

That makes sense, I said.

It seems you are caught up in mercy, he said.

I don't know, I said. I think I just want the world to be smaller.

But that is mercy, too, yes? To be sooner and closer to the ones you love?

Just to find one of them. I just want to find one of them.

Evan smiled. I was struck. He moved relentlessly. Hand over hand, pushing the wheels along. I thought, at first, that this relentlessness was something closer to violence. Maybe there was anger at the heart of him. But it seemed more like gentleness. Or, if not that, then directness. He wanted to get to the center of things. He wasn't in a hurry, but he was relentless. He reached into a canvas bag strapped to the side of his left wheel and pulled out a tennis ball. He threw it into the long grass, and Oslo hopped off his lap and ambled after it. I didn't ask why Evan had a tennis ball. It just made sense.

Why did you become a monk, he said.

It had nothing to do with God, I said.

Something someone obsessed with God would say.

No, no. I just wanted to get out of the city. I couldn't find myself there.

Find yourself? Oh, come on.

I don't know, I said. It sounded good coming out of my mouth.

Well, Evan said, what was it?

As he said this, he flipped a switch on his right wheel, and his wheelchair reclined like a La-Z-Boy. Even the foot rests popped up. He put his hands behind his head and waited for me to respond.

Oh wow, I said.

Well, he said.

I told him about Stu and the ten-year plan. I told him about the big buildings and the slogans, and the way that the business school students worshiped a neon ticker that ran around and around a glass-walled room. I told him about silently printing my insignificant papers on religion and watching them erupt in complete and utterly silent cacophony, their bodies bending and breaking, their faces awash in artificial light. I told him about not knowing what to do in such a world, and how I felt despair because of it, and how my despair grew the more I thought about it, because I assumed no one would understand, or that they would understand and say so what. I told him about the chocolate bread in my hands and the soft sounds of morning, the gentle chatter of people waking, these tiny gifts I wanted to hold forever, but couldn't. And I told him about my name.

Bobby, Evan said.

Haven't heard it in a while, I said.

Bobby, my brother, he said.

Odd to hear, I said.

And what about anything isn't just a bit fucking odd, Evan said.

He paused.

And what about anything isn't wildly weird, Evan said.

He paused again.

And what about anything does anyone know, Evan said.

Exactly, I said. Most days, I just wanted someone to begin each day by yelling *I don't know* at the top of their lungs. And then we'd all echo it back. That never happened.

For a long time, he said, I've thought life is an experiment in grace, and that most of us have failed because we think it is an experiment in something else. Grace is often confused with forgiveness, but the difference is that grace is bottomless. Forgiveness has its limits in human expectations. Grace is an exercise in the limitlessness of acceptance. It is what happens when you accept how conditional people are, and then move your heart toward the unconditional.

I don't understand, I said.

You do, Evan said. Even your statement—*I don't understand*—means you do.

What do you mean?

Look, you don't understand. Fine. That means you've placed a limit on what you know. Happens all the time. How often do you not understand?

I don't know. Always. Right now.

My point. Forgiveness is caught up in that. It's caught up in the limit of your understanding. But grace is like this invisible part of your heart that goes beyond that. It just fucking accepts that there's a limit to your understanding, and it reaches past that.

As he was saying this, he flipped his wheelchair out of La-Z-Boy mode and started zooming along, hand over hand on the wheel. I almost had to jog to keep up.

You see, he said. And I kid you not, he's zooming along as he said this.

You see, this chair might seem like a limit to my understanding. People might look at me and think that. But they don't know! My point is not that I am limitless. I am, in fact, very fucking limited. But I've accepted that. I don't know if other people ever get to that point.

How did it—

Happen? An 18-wheeler went right into the side of my car. Flying through an intersection. I could've been more cautious. I could've looked. But I was singing along to Edge of Seventeen.

Ah, I said.

I can forgive myself for that. But you know what?

Tell me, I said.

What I can't forgive is that I later found out that the 18-wheeler was hauling a load of Monsanto-poisoned apples, and that they all fell out when the crash happened. And people told me later that I was laying there, sprawled out, half-paralyzed, in a bed of poison apples that were already a waste, and there they were, going to waste again.

Jesus, I said.

Look, Evan said. We don't have enough models of the limitlessness of grace, the limitlessness of the good stuff. We have models of other kinds of limitlessness. You know, the people getting rich or dying as they tried. The people who say shit like all or nothing. The poor kid who pulls themselves up, as people say, by their bootstraps, and then pays their way to college and also knows how to play the trumpet and then becomes a model for all the good shit you can do with a life and then everyone who can't hang feels fucked. When I started rolling down this road, I was searching for more models of a different kind of limitlessness. One that was less about human achievement and more about humility.

Yeah, I said. You are searching for an alternative to the world we are told we are living in.

Exactly. It's funny. People think that me rolling across the country is an exercise in one kind of limit and another kind of limitlessness. They think it's all about endurance. Wow, they say. You're so strong. But it's not about that. It's about the limits of strength. My arms get tired. I have to rest. I am more aware of my body than ever. And so I extend it limitless grace.

That's beautiful, I said. Really.

Evan paused for a minute, pulled out a Gatorade bottle halfway filled with water the color of woodgrain, and then leaned his body over it and pissed into it. When he was done, he put the cap back on.

Why don't you?

Pour it out? You just never know. You really never know.

I tried to picture us from the eyes of those who drove past. At this point, my shirt was salt-dried, and as my arms swung past my body, these bits of salty dandruff would fleck off into the air.

My man, Evan said, we are either collective actors failing to enact a collective vision, or we are individual actors succeeding in enacting an individual version of some shodden collective.

Is that what you've learned, I said.

When my grandfather left Russia, he said, he had to dissolve all ties with the people he left behind. He settled in California. He learned how to be a tailor. He measured people's arms and legs. He had a small storefront. When I was a kid, he joked to me that he could stitch a secret pocket into my shirt if I needed a secret pocket. But he never stitched a secret pocket anywhere. He never had to. He lived a lonely life, but it was American. And then he died.

There was something missing, I said.

Life. Life was missing.

I don't know what you're getting at.

I'm saying that there has to be a right way to live. We don't see it here. The secret pocket my grandfather said he could sew. He never had to sew it, but he lived with the fear that he might always have to. There's a world of secret pockets full of contraband, and there's a world of secret pockets full of love. And that second world, it's not a secret.

It sounds beautiful.

It can be. It's not gone. It's not some fantasy we tell ourselves.

I know.

I'm saying, Evan said, we don't have to keep thinking about how to think of things. There are ways of life that make sense for all involved. We don't have to keep reinventing. There are beautiful models for how to be alive. But there are people in the way.

You were just talking about grace. I thought everyone deserves grace.

Even grace, Evan said, has its limits. Change one letter, and it becomes grave.

Okay, poet, I said.

Oslo tired and hopped in Evan's lap. We paused near a picnic table set up alongside a row of roadside stores. Pizza shop. Tobacco outlet. Empty storefront. Evan reached into a bag beneath his seat for an orange. He offered me half.

What will you do, I said, if you can't find your different world?

I think I will just keep rolling, he said. I'll make my own that way.

And what about you, he said. What if you don't find your brother?

I don't know, I said. I guess I'll just find a new place to live in and then leave. No. That doesn't make any sense at all. The truth is that I really don't know.

But what if, like you just said, this is all there is?

I thought of Brothers Levine and Levis. I thought of Father Stilts. I thought of Patti. I was getting close to understanding it now. There's only so much change you can expect. At a certain point, you have to commit to your place within this place. To your daily act of witness. Your bread-making, your listening, your going-out-to-look-at-the-moon. And you make of that your life. People get tired of hearing that there's somewhere better than where they are. So they try to make where they are better. They wake up and stack the biscotti. Was it good? Bad? I didn't say anything to Evan.

Can I read you something, Brother Bobby, Evan said.

Of course.

He took out his journal and flipped through it. He found the page.

Meditation beside a sewer beside the road, he said.

> *Someone made this ground, but they didn't make this water. Someone moved the water from a place it lived to a place where it then had to go. Someone is responsible for this. It's not me. It's not God. But someone. Just like where this road goes. Someone stood between here and there, and then they built it—*
> *The Between. All we see, everywhere, is desire. An avoidance of stillness. A fake complexity to escape the complexity of people. There is no place now that is not The Between, and the world is all Point A and Point B, filled with people trying to get somewhere. The water was once only where it was. And then, someone had to make it go everywhere.*

That's beautiful, I said. Really.

I paused.

The between, I said. I stared out at the road ahead. I looked back from where we came. I made a great big gesture with my hand to indicate how big the between was.

The between, Evan said.

Isn't that where we always are, I said.

I guess so, he said. But also, no. There are many betweens we live in. Yes. Yes, that's it. And sometimes we call everything a between when we don't have to, just like we call things an ending when they are not. Beginnings we wrongly name beginnings. Breathe. Meditate. Life's a t-shirt. How many t-shirts! How many t-shirts! The road to glory will lead to another road. The train will stall in the station and we will be told to get on another.

He was really animated now. He pushed his chair back from the table and gave the wheels six strong turns and then I was jogging again beside him. He kept going.

Our world, he said, wants us to stay on the fucking road, because anyone who has any power knows that's where they can keep us! To keep us as lost souls! Herding! Toward! Some proclaimed! Good! When they keep us there, we lose our power! We can't do anything. We tell ourselves to love the in between. We meditate to keep our anxious minds at bay. We don't have to do that! We can find a here right here. We don't have to always be going there.

But isn't that all talk, I said.

You're the monk, he said. You tell me.

I don't know if that makes me qualified to tell you anything. And if it did, I left the monastery.

I know, Evan said. But you still tried. I respect that. You tried to find a place where human complexity didn't have to live in service of some material aim. Listen. Are you listening?

I'm listening, I said, as I trotted next to him.

A month ago, I rolled by this house on the side of a road. A woman was hanging up string lights in her big yard, full of trees. It was more of a field. A field can be anything, you understand? We say yard, and we get certain ideas. But when you call something a field, the imagination has some fun with that. She saw me. Didn't balk. Didn't gawk. She invited me inside. Helped lift my chair over a little curb. Gave me a beer, asked where I was going. Asked where I was from. I told her about the poetry and the journey, about my search for something outside of society within society. I told her about the truck and the apples and the way I sprawled in the road, a pose I don't fucking remember, because I couldn't feel it, and because all of memory is feeling. She must have been almost 50. Bright beautiful eyes. When I told her that, those eyes got real wide and full of wetness. She asked if she could hug me, and I let her hug me. She told me she lost her only daughter in a car crash. Said she cried for a week. Sat at a table and cried. And then she put out an ad on the internet, inviting strangers who had lost someone—for any goddamn reason—to camp out in her big field. And people came. I'm telling you. They really did. She told me how they made a fire and grilled peaches and talked about their grief or they avoided talking about their grief because everywhere else they lived and worked and spoke only offered reminders of their grief. And they'd talk forever and then they'd leave and then they'd come back. She was always having people come and go. Even then, while she was talking, I heard the sound of a guitar coming from the back of the house. I asked. She wheeled me back there. And man. She took me back there. And how can I tell you? There were people there. They were sitting and someone passed me a cigarette and wheeled me right into their circle and I sat there all night and listened to the music. And no one asked because no one had to, because there was such real peace, man, and I told my story, once again, about the apples and truck, and finally, for the first time, someone fucking laughed. They laughed. And I laughed, too. And I realized that that's all I had wanted to do for a long time. Because it's a brutal story, and it's my life story, and I feel so much rage about the whole fucking thing, but I can't have my life be only rage. I have to laugh. I have to. And there was a fire. And the fire did that thing, you know? Where the sparks? Where they float up into the sky? And then disappear? It did that. And I slept out there, with my roof pulled over my head and my chair reclined. I didn't want to leave. Why isn't the world like that forever? It's not that hard, is what I'm saying. It makes me so mad.

He stopped rolling and sat there, breathing.

I was silent for a while. I wanted to know why it always took loss to bring people close. What did that say about the world, that it always took loss to break the barrier of our whatever—our selfishness, our meanness, our anger?

Why didn't you stay, I said.

He looked at me and seemed so old, just then, before turning young again.

I thought I had more to see, he said. That was just a precursor to some even greater beauty. I didn't want to be done yet.

But isn't that—

I know. I'm a hypocrite. Fucking sue me. I'm always in between, too. I believe, sometimes, in what I criticize. I get scared. People are complex.

I know, I said.

They're finicky.

Yes.

And fickle.

Sure.

And self-obsessed.

True.

And we've got these egos, man.

Yes.

Evan took a deep breath.

I'm torn, he said. There's a part of me that wants a world that can hold the bigness of that field. That world can be a field. A space for our imagination. Not a yard. Not something already decided. Something we have to mow with our John Deere tractors every Saturday like clockwork animals. I want the world of the field. A world of odd shit, strangeness. And grace. Children in the grass, making up games as they go along. And then there's a part of me that says, well, fuck it. I'll make my own world if it doesn't already exist.

You sound like a capitalist.

Sure. Yeah. Sure.

I'm sorry—

No, man, he said. It's true. Maybe that side of me is both the most human thing and the least. When we are young, we want to defeat everyone around us, and when we are old and full of loss and saggy, we claim victory by giving no fucks at all.

There's an in-between.

Hah.

No, really, I said. There is. The grace you mentioned. Maybe you apply it to yourself, and you hold it there. And you expand. And you get really, really big. In this invisible way. You get big enough to hold all the possible worlds. Not to understand them. Just to hold them. You know, like a rock in the light.

Maybe, he said. And then what?

Does it matter? Maybe you just live.

We traveled for a long time after that. Past gas stations and homes and one RV park. A dog chased us but then saw Oslo looking back—tongue out, one eye closed—from Evan's lap and stopped. A cat sunned itself on a porch, paw in its eyes. In the tall grass along a dirt road, a radio station hummed, shooting out songs from its one lonely antenna. *Are you alright. Are you alright.* I felt my skin pulled tight around the bones of my face. I felt my eyes grow wider. I could see everything in pure, arresting detail. The streaks of clouds. The little, brilliant yellow of the inside of each daisy that grew alongside the road.

I was just a kid when Billy was born. And when I held him in my arms for the first time—one of my nascent memories—I don't think I knew anything about fragility. About the bigness of smallness, the way so many tiny things are so easily broken, and the way the breaking matters so much. I haven't held a baby since, but I think, if I did, I would be much more scared than I was all those years ago. Somehow, in the years since then, I've become clumsier. A life builds, and builds, and builds. And you look back and only see the fault lines. Nothing seems purer than a child holding a child. But me, now, holding a child? That would be like an earthquake holding porcelain. I would go back to that moment at the cost of anything. That moment of holding Billy. I'd go back to feel the roots of love, those first moments before the world got in the way. Those nerve endings jumping across the gap to say *we are linked, no matter the world, no matter the breaking.*

Billy Keene

I have a treatise on family. It goes like this. Blood is a thing you cannot choose. Some say that makes it important. I say it means nothing other than what it means. That you cannot choose it. Blood is also magic. Some use the word magic to mean something that is completely good. I use it to mean that it does things that are hard to explain. If someone holds a deck of cards in front of your face and says pick one and then you pick one and then they say put it back and you put it back then they throw all the cards on the ground and gather them up and do a somersault and leap off the Empire State Building and still survive and then stand again in front of you holding the card you picked, then that's magic. It is not good or bad. It's just something you cannot explain. Blood is like that. You are born with a limited number of facts: you are alive, these people birthed you. None of that means more than it does, but it also means more than it does. One of the people who helped make you drives away in a lemon-yellow car and does not look back. One of the people who helped birth you sometimes screams at you and then you get sad, and you stammer, you grow forgetful, you feel mistaken, you feel odd in a way that feels impossible to justify. And yet, despite these facts, the fact of leaving and the fact of the screaming, the hitting, the yelling, you still feel a slight pull toward them. No, it's not slight. It's of the universe, like the tides. A massive pull beyond description. You want to run after the car that leaves. Hold the man who hurts you. What causes this other than magic? Blood is a thing you cannot choose, but it holds you. Damnit it does. And so my treatise on family is like this. Well, there's more. Some people might say, given the facts, that what is bound by blood is like a rubber band. You can stretch as much as you want, but you are still tied to what you're stretching from. Sure. I don't disagree. Maybe that's blood. No matter how far you stretch, you are still connected to what you are connected to by blood. But family is different. Imagine that rubber band stretched into a circle. Imagine you doing it. Imagine how hard. To stretch that band into a circle. To do it by your own volition. And so my treatise on family is also about that. If blood is what keeps you bound by rubber to that band of others, then family is who you stretch the band around. Who you decide to let in. And before you think about how trite that sounds, before you think that, remember how hard it is to stretch the band. Remember how hard it is to pull yourself away from what magic says you can never fully understand. And then remember how hard it is to draw a circle on a piece of paper. Remember how hard you tried? To draw a perfect circle? Hand shaking in the first-grade classroom? Remember that? But you draw it anyway. You end up making a circle that fits around your family. You end up making it perfect. Even if it takes all day. All night. Years. And you remember, too, that the formula for the shaded area of a circle is p, r, squared. And you remember your math teacher saying that even pi, that strange number, was an approximation that took a thousand years to make. And so everything is an approximation. That is part of my treatise on family. That there is the certainty of blood and the approximation of family. It's hard to move in the world. If you can move a circle around anyone, for the shortest amount of time, then that is a great thing. If you can escape the magic, if you can explain it. If you can say the card you are holding is the card I am holding. Guess what! There are two cards, and they are the same. There's no magic. This is exactly what it is. That is part of my treatise on family, too. That you should be able to say what it is, and why. Blood is not like this. I want to run away from the sadness caused by blood. I want to run and run. I want to stretch my rubber band around another group of people. Whoever. Part of my treatise on family is that living is hard. It is important, because of this, to do something that is your own. I do not fault the person who gets in a rowboat and rows across the ocean to make the wide circumference of the world. Why not? Look how large he is making his circle. Look how large his family could be.

A Father's List of Things, Continued

four picture frames, cardboard on their corners, still with their
stock photos of anonymous children
a pair of baby hands, painted blue, pressed against a wall
a shoebox full of medals
a dozen cans of condensed milk
two bags of Halloween candy, bite sized Reese's, one half eaten
Rand McNally Road Atlas, fraying at the corners
the phone that never rings
and next to it, a stack of unopened letters
one VHS tape of *The Last Waltz*, rewound to the exact moment
when Garth Hudson appears on stage with a saxophone during
the song "It Makes No Difference"
the picture Billy drew in kindergarten
the picture is of a house
a square filled with rectangles, with a triangle perched on top
in the picture, everyone is standing outside the house

Brother Keene

Somewhere along the way we wandered into a cemetery. It was one of those small-town ones, a crop of headstones among the daisies. There was a slight rise to the land, and the headstones stood above the field. They caught the light, though old, and they glittered. My eyes found them because of the glitter. I didn't think anyone would be there, and Evan wheeled off the road and pulled himself up the cinder climb that wound between the grass. Just at the top, we saw a car on the cemetery's other side, its door opened, and someone standing beside it, leaning against a building that looked barely big enough to fit a horse. It, too, was built from stone. It, too, glittered.

We held up a hand—just to do it, a formality. And a hand raised itself in return, and then it moved. A twitch of the fingers, beckoning us over.

I guess we're going over, Evan said.

We went through the cemetery. I touched each headstone that we passed. Just something soft, as if I was Moses walking between some people who really respected Moses. You know, just a gentle touch on the shoulder. To let them know I cared.

Jack, the man said.

Keene, I said.

Evan, Evan said.

Oslo, I said, and pointed.

Jack nodded at each of us. He held out a hand to Oslo, who lapped it immediately. I marveled at how quickly Oslo had grown, how he had once run from any movement. Now, he stayed.

So, Evan said. What is this?

This used to be my father's cemetery, Jack said. His name was Jack. My father's name was Jack. My name, as I said earlier, is also Jack. I'm not used to seeing people here.

It's beautiful, Evan said.

Really, I said.

I come here every day, Jack said. I make sure nothing fell over. That happens. The headstones. They fall over. They're narrow. The wind doesn't stop. And sometimes kids come and hide between them and play war games.

Awful, Evan said.

They paint their faces. They crouch down. Some are Nazis, some are American. They use the headstones as cover. They dig trenches. They do the whole bit.

Terrible, Evan said.

They use paintball guns. Pellets of paint. I come in the morning and the graves are red and green and blue and yellow.

Jesus, Evan said.

It's fine, Jack said. They're kids. It's all fine. I say hello to my friends.

He pointed as he spoke.

There's Anthony, this Greek man who ran the diner where my dad would eat. He'd tell mom he was going for a walk, but then he'd just go to Anthony's. Anthony once won an award for Americanism from the local Lion's Club. And there's Tommy, who cut my mom's hair, not my dad's, though my dad would go sometimes—before or after Anthony's—to talk to Tommy about town. Who was born and who died and who got hurt and did you hear and did you know. And there's Marcie, the waitress who worked at the Flagpole. She worked there even through the dialysis treatment. A decade of it. That was someplace different. Where mom and dad would go to eat their salad wraps and drink these big rum and cokes. Marcie got buried in the track pants she wore each night while working. I can still hear the *swish* of them.

Your friends, Evan said.

My family, Jack said.

And your dad, I said.

Jack looked at me and I saw his eyes for the first time and there was a brutal weight to them. It was as if an invisible, insanely small animal was hanging on for its life on the bottom of his eyelids, pulling them down to the depths.

He had a pain in his stomach, Jack said. He didn't like the doctor. He ate Tums like candy but it didn't help. I don't know why it would. I didn't say anything. I bought some for him. More than once. Even now my glove compartment has three bottles of them. Chalky pellets. Yeah, candy. And he waited and waited. He waited when he coughed blood. He waited when he doubled over beside the car beside the road. When we finally drove him to the hospital and they ran the tests, they said it was time, and my dad asked me to put his body where he worked.

He looked over at one particular headstone that seemed almost smooth, sanded down along the edges. Easy to the touch. Like you could place your hand against it and it would feel like part of your body.

And you put him here, I said.

Not at first, Jack said.

What, Evan said.

No, no. I couldn't, Jack said.

He shook his head, put his fingers in his eyes, squeezed the bridge of his nose.

Well, he said, what the hell.

He said this as if to himself. Like Evan and I were two birds perched on a branch above his head, eavesdropping on the sometimes-bit of pain that life sometimes is.

I took him from the morgue, he said.

What, Evan said.

I took him from the morgue. I snuck in, middle of the night. I had the spare key. Undertaker knew me. I took him from the morgue in the middle of the night and put him in the back of my car.

This car, I said.

This car. I put him there in the back. Sat him up. Threw a bottle of Tums his way. Talked to him. Told him we were going on a journey. Took 81 all the way north. Past the state line, past Corning. Took him to one of the Great Lakes. Forget which. Erie. Ontario. It's all a blur. Stopped once at a Wendy's and bought him a Junior Bacon Cheeseburger and just tossed it back there for him to eat if he wanted. Asked him if he was hungry. Told him to be sure to eat his Tums. After the burger, you know. Got to the lake's shore, and I skipped stones for an hour. I kept talking to him, even though he was in the car, probably couldn't hear.

Even though, Evan said.

Even though he was dead. I talked to him nonstop. I said you wouldn't believe, dad. I said you have no idea. I said I miss you already. I said I wish, I wish, I wish.

He was crying now. Jack. He was pouring tears from the big reservoirs of those heavy eyes. And all the while I thought how all of this had happened while I might have been on a bus, or sitting up in bed. Huge spectacle of grief amidst the ordinary. A gust of wind blew Jack's hair across his eyes and sent one single tear out into the air, where I imagined it landed right beneath a sunflower, and shot that sunflower straight into the clouds.

I'm sorry, I said.

I had to bring him back, Jack said. And I did. I brought him back.

Is that a crime or something, Evan said.

Jack laughed the kind of laugh that just sounds like breath.

I think so, Jack said. A body across state lines.

You're a rockstar, Evan said.

I had to do it, Jack said. There wasn't some other choice in my brain. It wasn't that or else. It was just that. I grew up among the dead. I just couldn't accept it.

Some headstones had sayings etched into their faces. Family man, one said. Remembered for love and nothing else, another said.

Live forever in heaven.

I talked to someone for a bit, Jack said. They told me that my grief was like a ball bouncing in a room. They said in the room was one of those cartoon switches that drops a bomb. A big red button. They said the ball is always bouncing. And they said that most days, the ball bounces and doesn't hit the button. But then, they said, it'll be a blue-sky Sunday, and the ball will hit the button, and you'll be on your knees crying. People will think you saw a ghost. That's what grief is like. It gets you any second. The ball is bouncing always. And life is just adding more of those red buttons as you go.

He laughed again. Another breath.

I guess you can tell it's been a while since I've seen people, he said.

Evan's got a question for you, I said.

I do, Evan said. Wait. I do?

You do, I said.

Shoot, Jack said.

Evan looked at me and I looked at him and there was Oslo, perched again on his lap, squinting his one-eyed squint across the wide ocean of the world.

Well, Evan said, seeing as you're our ferryman shepherding us to the unknown realm of death, I want to know, since it's been on my mind. I want to know: how should we live?

Breath-laugh. Smile of surprise. Sunlight glittering the stones.

I come here each day, Jack said, and make sure nothing has toppled over. It's not always fun, but it's my small field that I tend to. If you're lucky enough that you've been given a small field, I think you tend to it. I think that's how you live. But why would you ask me?

Look at your field, I said.

There were lilacs blooming between the stones. These brilliant blitzes of purple that sucker-punched the heart and made me believe in what was possible. I couldn't see them from the road. I had to be here, in the field, looking with care. And when I did, all that care that Jack had put in exploded through the field of my vision, and even in this place of death, there was this music of sight—purples and yellows and reds speckled amongst the glittering grey of the headstones that said the names of mothers and fathers and kid and people loved and forgotten and maybe even hated, but still cared for. Gentle Jack, rubbing the stains away.

Will you do me a favor, Jack said.

Anything, we both said.

Jack reached into his car and picked up a gallon bag filled with pebbles. There must have been dozens. A hundred. Smooth and jagged. All sorts of different shapes and sizes.

I filled this bag on the shore, when my dad was in the backseat. I filled a bunch of bags. Will you take this one? Take it around? Put a stone or two on each grave? I want people to think this is a place that is visited.

And so we did. Evan held the bag in his lap, and we moved between the graves for an hour, placing a pebble atop each headstone. Sometimes two. The grass was a uniform height. All of it. Maybe three inches. Maybe Jack mowed it every other day. We put two stones on Anthony's. Two stones on Tommy's. Two stones on Marcie's. We found a grave for a dog—*May you have all your treats in heaven*— and tried to put a stone in Oslo's paw and have him place it on the marker. It didn't work. We put three stones on that grave. When we were done, Jack was right. The place looked like a visited thing.

Thank you, Jack said.

And then we walked away. We walked down the cinder path that ran between the cemetery and looked back up at the headstones, tall, risen things topped with pebbles, as if they had grown three stories since we'd seen them last. It seemed some kind of cosmic justice that people who couldn't run away were visited by those who could. But there was also something beautiful about choosing not to run, about staying put. About running with your father and then bringing your father home to care for him.

The heart is never just a heart, I said.

Evan looked at me.

What's that, he said.

Something a monk told me.

A heart is never just a heart, Evan said.

What do you think he meant, Evan said.

And there, standing next to me, was Brother Levis. He was munching on biscotti. He was wearing his long garment. His eyes had the same look to them that I'm sure they always had but that I never missed enough to see. Like bays at low tide—all this vastness, exposed.

You've been walking for a long time, Brother Levis said.

I have been, I said. I left right after we talked.

And have you found him?

He looked around, nodded, and answered his own question.

No, I said. But I met a woman who saves dogs. She smoked cigarettes. She said a beautiful blessing. I baked her a loaf of bread. I met this man who is rolling his body across the country in search of something that is not this country. I have a dog now. I think.

So you've met more of your life.

How do you do that? Make my life sound like something mystical?

Because it is, Brother Levis said.

I smiled. I missed him. I missed Patti, too. I missed my father. I missed my mother. I didn't know what to miss of Billy, but I wanted to find him so I could tell him that I missed him.

Do you miss anything, Brother Levis?

Of course I do, he said. But I do not think of missing as something that is not part of life. If I miss something, it is with me. The Bible says *we did not miss anything when we were in the fields, as long as we went with them.*

But you are not with those you miss, I said. In fact, you are far away.

But I am, he said. Widen your idea of the field, Brother. If you widen it large enough, it can contain all that you miss, and all that you miss will be there with you, in the same field.

But how can I do that? If I can only see so far?

Stop, he said. Breathe. No, actually. Breathe. Let everyone walk away. Go on, let them. Notice how small you are. How huge this thing is that goes on around you, and how much you do not know of it. There, did you see that? The bird soaring across the daytime moon? Do you see it now? If you are small, then those you miss and love must be small, too. They must be like little things in this big and wide thing we call the world. And if they are small, and you are small, then the world must feel big but must not be so big that it cannot contain each of you. It must be like one field, this world. You must believe that. We built the roads that cut through the fields. We drew the boundaries. We divided ourselves among the things we divided. Unbuild the roads in your mind. There, wherever you are, you are among each other. Even if you have not found each other, you have found each other.

But it's hard, Brother.

A heart, he said, is never just a heart. A life is never just a life. If anything was only what it was, then you could call something easy, and it would be easy.

He vanished, then, and left a crumb of biscotti by his feet. I looked at Evan. He had wheeled a hundred yards ahead. I jogged to catch up.

I think he meant, I said, that it's okay for everything to feel as much as it feels.

And if you feel too much?

Maybe you're doing it right, I said.

I doubt so much, Evan said. My hands. Fucking blistered from turning these wheels. When the midday road starts burning, my wheels get hot, and everything burns. I thought all this wandering would lead me somewhere. I thought all this pain would lead me somewhere, too.

Maybe you demand too much of you, I said. Not just the world.

Yeah, Evan said.

I'm serious, I said. Look at you. You're hard on the world, but you're harder on yourself. You're all blistered and calloused. There's a bite to you that's beautiful, but sometimes, I think, you're biting yourself.

It's because all the apples are rotten, Evan said.

I smiled, then, and looked at him. He was ruddy and shiny at the same time. He looked like something just pulled up from earth and catching the sun for the first time. A mess of dirt, but beautiful. Newly grown. Out of this world.

Fucking wreck, I said.

He smiled, then.

Both of us, he said. Fucking wrecks.

A car drove by and screamed the long scream of some big machine hurtling at ninety miles an hour, and the world returned in all of its noise.

I've been thinking, Evan said.

That you should go back, I said.

He nodded.

To the woman with the lights, I said.

He nodded again.

Then go, I said. Turn around and go. Say you met me. Call it God's plan.

He laughed. Then his eyes grew wide. Then they blinked rapidly—ten, twenty times. Then they grew wide again, and filled with tears. The world was full of tears.

It's just, he said. I thought I could make it simple, man. I thought

I could go out and find it. And that it would be there, shining, and waiting. That I wouldn't have to think. That it would present itself as right.

But Evan, I said. It did.

It really did, didn't it?

Go, I said.

Turn, I said.

Just fucking go, I said.

He gripped his wheels and I saw the cut-up jagged skin of his hands, blistered and pus-filled and bulbous and shining in the light. And then he turned the chair around.

It was fun, he said.

His back was to me. He was wheeling away. He was reclining his head back. He was shouting his voice toward me but it looked like he was shouting up toward the heavens.

It was fucking fun, he said again. People don't talk about that enough. Amidst all the bullshit. They don't say that whatever you find should also be fun.

He laughed this big, loud, cackling laugh. Something bigger than both of us. And I turned around with that laugh a wild echo in my ears. And I began to walk away. I held the tennis ball in my hand. I looked at it, damp thing, no longer neon, almost the color of the earth with these circles of light shining through it all, as if it radiated light despite all the use. Oslo stood next to me, looking at it too, mouth open, long spit of drool. Happy guy. What was this life? When you put yourself in it, so much shit happens. I turned back around, and I waited until Evan looked small enough in the distance to be covered by my outstretched hand. And then I rubbed Oslo behind his right ear, mouthed the word *goodbye,* and threw the ball down the road.

Billy Keene

Shit. Happiness. Sadness. Sorrow. Joy. Double-tied knots. How to make a fire. Seven million names of trees. Every reason I ran away. My mother. My father. My brother. So much. Sometimes, sitting alone, waiting for Dad to come home, I logged onto the computer and pretended I was someone I was not. I was a woman tired from working, needing someone to talk to. I was younger than I was. I was older. I was ancient. I lived in the woods. I lived on the 90th floor of the tallest building in the biggest city. The thoughts of every person, what do they become? Answer: purple light at sunset. Forty different creation stories. history. Why, when people say history, do they pretend to know so much? Why do people pretend? Anxiety. Fear. Weather. Teachers who think they know everything. I want a weatherman who laughs and says *fuck this*. It is hard, just to be alive. Say it! More people should say it! Listen to the sounds of birds. There are as many of them as trees. Seven million plus one. Each of them singing. Let's all listen together.

High Five and Whaleman go up the trail and leave me with Doctor. I am tired and Doctor knows it and we sit for a little while. High Five says they will find camp a few miles up. High Five says we can meet them there. She says there is a little rise up ahead and then a bigger drop and then after that, a road, and then after the road, a camp. She rubs her knuckles that spell her name. She smiles. For a brief second, I wish she is my sister. I want her to hold me small and tight. To laugh the way girls laugh when they find the whole world funny. A mouth wide open laugh. I like High Five for that. She is always smiling. When she leaves us, she is smiling, too. She and Whaleman walk and they look like they are laughing at something. Doctor sits quiet and then looks away from me and says you don't ever have to explain yourself. I say I know. I say I wasn't planning on it. Doctor says I mean it, and I pull a leaf off a branch and make it into the shape of Texas. Doctor says I've seen so many people wheeled into rooms without explanation. They just woke up one day and had a heart attack or got beat or went through with the thing they thought about doing but never did, until they went through with it and almost died. And then they got wheeled into a room with me and I tried to save them even though I had never met them before. Do you know what I mean, Wondering? That's what Doctor asks. He shakes his head. I throw my leaf away. I think there is a great big gap between every person on earth and I have no idea how to make it less than big. Sometimes I feel there is a great big gap between myself and myself. Who I am is one lost thing walking from one part of me to the next.

How to get from here to there: find a stick, crouch down, put your forehead on it, spin around twenty times, let go of the stick, try to walk without falling, meander, disco dance, curse, scream, laugh, curse again, keep going, keep going somewhere, say where am I, say where are you, tell yourself you're not going to ask for help, admit that you probably will have to, have you fallen yet, how about now, or now, or now, and now that you have regained your balance, wonder if maybe are you lost, because, if you are, you're probably there.

I saw my dad naked once. I saw my dad sad. I saw my dad sit alone in the car outside the house when he came back from work. I saw my dad take one CD out of the car's CD player and put another CD in. I saw my dad hesitate. I saw my dad smile. I saw my dad take off his belt. I saw my dad not know he was being seen. I saw my dad coach a baseball team. I saw my dad do the laundry. I saw my dad make a tomato sandwich. I saw my dad carry the bag home from the diner and open the bag and hand me the food he ordered for me. I saw my dad say nothing for a long time. I saw my dad perform the motions of a life. I saw my dad wake and piss and change and leave and come back and eat and sleep. I saw my dad answer the phone. I saw my dad let the phone ring. I saw my dad smile in polite conversation. I saw my dad rub the bridge of his nose. I saw my dad alone in another room holding his forehead in his hand. I saw my dad look at me and then look through me. I saw my dad look at me hard. I saw my dad wonder. I saw my dad rage. I saw my dad clench the wheel of the car. I saw my dad not even try to see where he was going. I saw my dad mistake someone for someone else. I saw my dad cycle through the channels. I saw my dad have a hard time deciding. I saw my dad fill up the car. I saw my dad stand there and seem to enjoy it. I saw my dad trying hard to smile. I saw my dad trying hard. I saw my dad fail. I saw my dad look at me with love. I saw my dad unsure of himself. I saw my dad not know how to be alive. I saw my dad pretend. I saw my dad.

Doctor and I go walking up the ridgeline. It seems we are walking into the sky. The way the trees separate themselves for us. Sometimes I wonder how it happened. I wonder about the trees, the birds, the sky. I wonder about chance, and how long it took chance to happen. I wonder sometimes about beauty and why we like it. Why some things are beautiful and some are not. I wonder so often. Wondering, Doctor says, what will you do when you get to the end of this trail. I think. I don't talk. I didn't know that there was a real end. In my mind it all goes on forever. I don't want to make a choice. I don't say anything. I shrug. Doctor shrugs too. He says I guess we have time. He says I guess we will figure it out. I think he's right. I haven't thought about anything beyond right now, how it feels good to be a heart with people who have hearts. How it feels good to be with them and eat with them and listen to Doctor hum as he falls asleep. Doctor looks back at me like he's going to ask a question. It is just when the ridge drops down in a steep way. Doctor's foot goes for a rock and misses it. Doctor slips and falls. He tumbles head over body, feet in the air. He disappears from the top of the ridge, where he once was, and I hear a thud. I scamper over the top and look down to him. There is blood on his forehead and his right foot is facing a different direction than usual. He looks at me with something between a smile and a grimace. Wondering, he says, I'll be fine. You need to run to Whaleman and High Five. I'll need to be carried up to camp. I'll need to be carried somewhere, wherever. I just stare at him.

His blood so dark it is almost blue. Wondering, he says again, and he is about to laugh I think because it is the kind of thing only he can say at only the right time. I need you to run, he says. Trust me, he says. I'm a doctor.

When I run I feel endless. When I run I feel fast. When I run I feel not as tired by the world. When I run I feel not as sad. When I run I feel like someone who is really good at talking, talking. When I run I feel like someone who is really good at anything doing that thing. When I run I feel the split second moment when the ground is not a thing I touch. When I run I feel like held there for longer than a split second. When I run I feel the tiny spring of my legs loading and then lifting. When I run I feel the smallest lean of my body. When I run I feel seen by myself. When I run I feel the air buffing the space right above my cheeks. When I run I feel, sometimes, tears. When I run I feel like I could go on until I can't. When I run I feel like I could go on. When I run I feel like I do not have to stop. When I run I feel like the tip of a pencil as an invisible hand draws a line across a page. When I run I feel like wind must feel when it rustles a blade of grass and then another. When I run I feel like the little loop below a lowercase cursive g. When I run I feel like I could go on, like I'll go on.

And so I run. I leave my bag at Doctor's feet. I have not run since the race. It takes me all of two seconds to learn again. I quick-step down the descent. I gather speed. I feel myself once again becoming myself. The blur of trees to my right. The little language of legs. The way I know how the ground will feel before I touch it. I feel the light grace of my feet. The liftoff that follows next. I hang my arms loose by my side. I am who I am. Just a boy, running. No ties, no needs, no burden beyond the gentle burden of the next step. I am only who I am in this moment. No past, no history. I have not run away. I have not run from. I have not escaped. I am just a boy running through the woods. The light dapples my arms. Little shadows come and go. Leaves brushed through, a faint scratch on my leg. I am just a boy running through the woods. The trail flattens out. I can run forever like this. The earth soft beneath my feet, somewhere distant to be, the love of being needed. I don't want to be rescued. I am just fine as I am. I am soft and strong as wood. I can bend without breaking. Hear me, little birds. Hear me, big world. My footsteps make a hush. I can hush all night, wonder my way through the world. The trees diverge to make a clearing. Three steps up, and then a road. I look once to my left and then to my right. Full stride. Whaleman and High Five up ahead. My stride opens up. I can feel that split second when I am flying. I am out in the open. I feel like I could go on, like I'll go on.

Brother Keene

I counted my money before I set foot in the Wawa. I had a hundred dollars left. The days had quickly eaten up my meager savings. Invisibly, almost. The two consecutive nights I had spent on motels. The hastily purchased snacks, a five-dollar bill pulled off the stack of bills with no thought about what would be left. Time away from money did that to money. It made it seem less precious, a slight annoyance-tax that had to be paid between two humans just to prove they had an interaction. To know I had spent so swiftly, and apparently so poorly—it made me feel alone.

In the Wawa, I spent too long standing at the touchscreen that contained within it an unlimited variety of custom sandwiches. I toggled my finger between the choice to add or withhold bacon for an extra dollar. I withheld it, with the hope that such a choice might offer me good fortune in some time to come. I ate my sandwich outside, unfolding the sacred map. I traced my finger along the highlighted line, found my intersection. I was nearing the end. I was in the hands of whatever angels from the past had once journeyed here. I would accept any god. I would follow any mystery. I began again to walk.

The funny thing about walking alone was that I never felt alone in a physical way. Sometimes I wanted more of it, that loneliness. I wanted a wind that would stop winding, birds that would stop birding. I wanted a hush that stayed hushed. But soon enough, whatever needed to be would simply start being, and I wouldn't be alone. I guess that's how it is. Life moves, wild and free and with or without you.

Years after my mom left, I went to see her in secret. She lived two states away, on the coast of the Atlantic. It was a distance that seemed, when I was young, to be insurmountable, but really was not that far. I left my house in the morning and took one bus and then another and then another. When I got to where my mom lived, she was standing right outside her front door, as if being a mother meant developing an awareness of where your child was and where they were journeying and when they would arrive. She was ready for me, is what I am trying to say. And she asked me if I wanted to go for a walk, and we did. She said she walked every morning, by the water. The morning breeze that day was more of a wind, and my hair flew across my eyes and the smallest bits of salt dangled from the tips of my eyelashes. I was in high school, skipping for the day. I felt guilty, and that feeling swelled in my gut when I thought about it, so I tried not to think about it. Instead, I looked at my mom, who seemed tinier than ever before, like someone who could've been blown away by a strong gust. I wanted to touch her shoulders for a minute, to make sure she was standing on both feet, and strong, but I hadn't touched her at all in so long.

We walked for a long time. My mom told me about how her walks would sometimes begin at dark. She would walk for miles through the night, the tips of ocean waves candle lit by stars, and then, after hours, she would see the sun come up all *slow and melty* out of the water. That's what she said. *Slow and melty*. I missed her tremendously the moment she said that. I didn't really know, before seeing her, how much I missed her. But I missed her then. It was the way she said it. The way she dwelled a bit on both words—*slow and melty*—as if she was chewing on them for sweetness before letting them escape her mouth. She sounded like a kid. She sounded like someone who had such a capacity for joy that it made me want to weep. I didn't realize it then, but later

I did—that part of what made that moment feel so special was that I was watching her become her own person. Gorgeous miracle of sonhood: I had witnessed my mother grow. When I thought of it later, the walk on the water, the thought of my mother in the dark, the slow and melty sun rising in the east, I wished it had lasted longer, that still-long but forever-too-short moment. I wished I had said *say it again, mom*. But nothing lasts longer than it lasts. Things are as long as they are. Or as short. I think the long and short come after. I think we use those words when we look back and wish we could've done something to alter time, to hang on. But we can't go back to hang on. We can't go back at all.

My mom said she walked as the sun came up and then turned around and walked home. She said it helped to see the sun, and when I asked what it helped, she just looked at me briefly—and I knew then that she was my mother—and looked away. A smile escaped her lips. And then her face became still and graceful and yet almost mad. She didn't answer me. We walked quietly together for an hour, the wind in our hair. As I walked alone, I thought of her. If what Brother Levis said was true, then she was walking with me, our closeness just a matter of perspective, my eyelashes covered with salt.

The world was something you dealt with every day. Making of it what you could. Each morning, my mom woke up and walked by the water and thought of those words—slow and melty—and maybe felt a little bit of a child rising up within her and joining her as part of herself. And maybe she held onto that feeling for as long as she could, the wind in her hair, the smell of salt. And maybe she did this for the same reason that Patti rescued dogs, or Jack tended the graves. Because she found some tiny place to be who she was, even when who she was felt lonely, or scared. There is the mystery we share and the mystery we have no idea how to share. I think the latter is almost impossible to address, and that we share, at the very least, in how we deal with that impossibility.

My mother walks along the ocean. Brother Levis stacks biscotti. Patti feeds the dogs.

Maybe the funny thing about walking alone was that I never really was alone. No matter the sounds of 18-wheelers hauling freight down the highway, or the occasional fox darting across the road. No matter the wind in my hair or the speckled white-purpleyellow petals of flowers that dotted the tall grass. I was my own self trying to reckon with my own self's particular mystery. Why it was that my own family split open like a flower in spring, and then shed each petal. Why it was that I could never seem to sit in one place for an extended period of time. Why, I thought, was the most beautiful question to ask, and also the most terrible. A question that is almost never answered to satisfaction, and then is repeated over and over. All of history is the sound of that word.

I never got to ask Brother Levis why. Why he carried on. Why he went away. Why he stayed away. Why he kept lingering in one spot, working for a god that might not exist. That's not true, though. It's not true that I never asked why. Saying it that way makes it sound like I would have asked, if only given the opportunity. But I had the opportunity. I just didn't ask. And so I asked.

Why, Brother Levis, I said.

And Brother Levis appeared.

Why what, he said. He smelled of flour and eggs. He brushed his hands against his tunic and left a faint dust. It was that dust—powdered against the black fabric—that made me believe he was real.

I just wanted to ask why, I said.

That cannot be true, he said. I wouldn't have journeyed here to answer such an unspecific question.

I wanted to smell his hands, to see if they smelled like almonds.

There is a why, he said, that can be applied to anything. And to anything there can be applied a why.

That makes it sound like everything has an answer.

I didn't say that, he said. I only said that we can direct our why toward anything.

I want to know the why of you, I said.

Still unspecific, he said. Try again.

He dusted off the flour from the sleeves of his tunic. The flour hung in the light like dust caught in a column of sunshine-gold beaming through a window.

I want to know why you are here on this earth, I said. Why you are doing almost nothing, remaining in the same place. I want to know why you left the house where you found your brother, where you lived, and why you never returned.

Who are you, he said, to say that I am doing almost nothing?

You're right, I said. That's an assumption.

A mind can play a million tricks before the body moves a single inch.

So you left the world to live inside your mind?

Is the mind a terrible thing to live within?

I'm always scared of mine.

That's because it's alive, he said.

A big bird flew above us, wings the size of humans. It flapped them once, and soared for forever.

So you're not scared, I said.

I didn't say that, he said. I have fear, too. My fear is part of life. And to be alive is to be in the world.

He was right. The mind lives inside the body which lives in the world. To be inside the mind was to be inside the world. It wasn't a prison or a dungeon or a scenic retreat. It wasn't limited to such ideas. I was walking alone and he was next to me. The sun cast his long shadow on the road, and he was as there as anyone could be. He was in my mind, which was the same as being in the world.

So you never left the world, I said.

No, he said. I needed to practice my grief.

But how? And why?

It felt, he said, and still feels, so powerful that I knew I could not teach myself to live without it. The older I grew, the less I wanted to. Sometimes a feeling is as true as a person. It walks beside you, tells you about the leaves. It remembers a time you forgot. My brother on a tire swing, and how it looped up and over the branch, and how he hung on the whole time, and never let go. I had to climb up to cut him down. Why learn to live without that? I wanted to be able to touch my grief, to make my feeling of loss as close to a feeling of being as I could. I devoted myself to ritual. I left the world of progress and found the world of belief. Belief for the sake of belief. The simplicity of trying to know what you cannot know, knowing that you will never know it. Belief is like grief. It is a loss happening in reverse, the mind working toward something that it cannot know with the knowledge that it cannot know it.

Where in the world—

Would I find that world? Nowhere but where I am.

He looked at me and smiled, and I thought of my mother. At some point, I realized, you had to accept. Accept something. Accept this life. All appearance and your own small reality, and the light shining through it.

You see, Brother Levis said, we are always telling ourselves one story or another about what we will find. Even the Bible. *Seek and you shall find.* It is as if finding is the goal, over and over again. Find the answer. Find the secret. Find your way through loss and come out on the other side, where loss is no more because you have found the way. But find me someone who has completely found themselves, and you won't find me anyone. My brother found himself. It was a choice he made, I imagine, because he decided he was too small for the world. He had a brief moment of certainty. The briefest moment, found on the other side of a long, enduring struggle. And he found an answer. And his answer was that the struggle would never end. His answer was that he was hopeless, and would be hopeless forever. He found himself hopeless, with that awful certainty. Which meant he found himself with no place to go. I keep him so close to me to try to find him there, in that lonely nowhere. I want to unfind him from that scared place, and turn him toward the sacred, which is where the world is, and where it is okay—always—to be uncertain. It is in that place where we can be together.

Even if you can't be together?

But we can. We can, you see. We can be together. We travel together at night, walking out of the paths we have walked ourselves into. I go out to the stars and he is beside me, as I am beside you, and he is playfully smoking a cigarette made of sugar. His laugh is in my ear. He is alive.

But where is the body, I said.

Why need the body? Just so Thomas can place his finger upon it and measure if it is real? The body might lead us to doubt more than the mind. You asked me why earlier. There is a home in the mind. There, I can spend an entire day seeking, and loving what I seek.

He produced a sprig of rosemary from the inside of his tunic and held it to his nose, and then to mind. It smelled as real as the lilacs on the side of the road.

Should I stop walking, I said.

What do you think, he said.

I just don't know what I'll find. Or if.

And is that okay? To not know? To encounter nothing? To encounter something that might dismay you?

I don't know yet, I said. I'm always not knowing.

Then it is okay, he said, because it is your life.

He vanished then, like snow un-falling itself from sky. And I missed him. I held my hand out in the air and closed my fist and thought I held a thimble full of flour, thought I felt the coarse grain of it falling between my fingers, but it was just the air we both had breathed.

And Patti was putting out food for the dogs, and they came running across the fields and the road and around the house. They came running like good dogs, like happy guys, like beautiful little spry-legged creatures who wanted and loved and played and fought and yipped and yelled into the air. Who licked the hand that fed them after running away from it at first, who learned to love, after great difficulty, anything that moved. And Evan was reclining in his chair, looking up at the sky and wishing he could sketch the one long strip of cloud that seemed to hang like pastry dough suspended in the air, warmed up from the descending sun so that it looked like an eclair, frosted on one edge. And he was rolling and looking and wishing and hurting and hoping that when he made it back to the house with the lights, there would be people there, and the sound of music, and maybe enough of a world for him to escape from the world—this one—for long enough to feel okay about anything, anything at all. And Oslo was in his lap, not worrying about anything other than the ball that sometimes soared over his head and bounced down the road or into the sunflowers beside the road. And he leapt off the lap that held him and gripped the ball with his teeth and tasted it and brought it back to Evan's lap, where he deposited it, damp and spongy and marbled with grit, and soon there was no clear distinction between the spit in Oslo's mouth and the spit that covered the ball, so that both things became one and the same, and that, holding the ball in his mouth, maybe Oslo felt he was holding himself, though I don't know if Oslo—a dog—could put it that way, but if anyone could, perhaps a dog would. And my father was tired of trying and tired of waiting and was trying to figure out how to live a life that now included yet another before and after. He was cataloging his belongings, rifling through the house, opening drawers, and that word—*belonging*—stretched in his mouth until it snapped and left him sobbing alone in the morning, not knowing until then how much loss is part of love. How many livings and leavings, he asked himself, make up a life? Isn't one enough? That is what my father was asking, and it was—I think—a worthy question, because of how gnawing it was, and devastating, and because of how such things that gnaw at us must be worthy of something, and because we are so often gnawing and feeling gnawed at that we are always trying to figure something out. And my mother was walking along the ocean, and looking at the ocean, staring into the endless mirror of a life remade. And my brother had to be somewhere among the trees, shining in the light that shone between the trees.

And a car pulled up alongside me. It felt like life happening again, even though life is always happening. A window rolled down, and a face appeared, pockmarked and cratered, decorated with the dusted stubble of a white beard. A finger emerged, too, and it pointed at my bag, which at that point was crinkled and stinking and faded by the sun. And a smile came, too, a lopsided one, like a half a face was forever dedicated to joy and joy alone. I looked down at my right shoe, so worn that my big toe had drilled a hole through it. And I looked back up, and still there was that face, that finger pointing at my bag, that smile. Still there was that smile.

Are you going to the trail, he said.

The trail, I said.

The trail, he said. The AT. Trailhead's up the road. You going there? I assume you are. I'm a trail angel. Certified. Been doing this years. No ID, I know. That proves it. If you're looking for that kind of thing. But I'm certified. I'll take you there.

And he reached over and opened the door and I got in the car, and I sat in the front seat of this Honda Civic that sort of rattled a bit as it sped down the road. This man—he started talking the moment he hit the gas. He told me about the years he had spent driving people to and from trailheads up and down the East Coast. He had a bobblehead of a beagle on his dashboard. He held a flip phone in front of me and said this bad boy still packs a punch, and my number gets around, and I never know at which hour of the night I might get a call from someone who needs a ride to a Wawa or a Holiday Inn Express or just needs to catch a lift an hour away from the trail to see someone they haven't seen in years.

He said that's my job. To provide that lift. Make someone's day. That's what he said: to make someone's day. And he smiled with that one side of his face as he said it, the front bumper of his Civic almost skidding along the road.

We sped down the road. We passed a Dollar General, a Wawa, and another. Sometimes that front bumper hit asphalt, and sparks flew. They looked, even in fading daylight, like stars.

I once stopped in the parking lot of that Dollar General, he said. Was taking someone to the train. He'd done a long stretch of the AT. Could tell. Smelled like an ass had an ass. Had no money. Had bought his train ticket before he got on the trail. Good lord he smelled so bad. I didn't care. But I pulled in that lot. Bought him a pack of baby wipes. Let him hide behind the car and get naked, wipe himself clean. I told him I didn't mind if he smelled, but you never know about the people on that train.

How many people have you driven, I said.

You're my 92nd. I keep an exact count.

He gestured toward the green notebook that sat below the bobbling beagle.

When I drop you off, I'll write it in this notebook. One slash. A single tally. You ever seen that movie? A bell rings, an angel gets its wings? I don't need to wait for wings. I have them. Every time I make a slash, my wings get bigger. They're so big now. Can't you tell? We're basically flying. It's a good feeling.

Why do you do it?

And he looked at me while he was driving. Both hands on the wheel. He looked at me and there were these wrinkles at the edges of his eyes that spread like milk cutting through a cup of coffee.

Had a kid in a school nearby, he said. Years ago. Had a kid in a school nearby and had a job. I went to work each day but before I did I waited for the bus to take my kid to school. It was a simple thing, but it was a life. It was today and then tomorrow and then the next. Wake up, wait, work, repeat. And I loved my kid. I loved how he stood waiting for that bus. Older he got, the more he said I didn't have to watch. But I watched. He had a backpack with a big bright yellow taxi on it. He held the straps of it as he waited.

He didn't take his hands off the wheel as he told me this, but I watched them grip round the wheel tighter, as if they were becoming the hands of his own son wrapped around the straps of a backpack.

That bag was too big for him, he said. Got bigger every year. Filled with books. I watched him all those years. I watched him each morning and he got smarter and taller every day. Felt like he wasn't much older than a baby, but goddamn he grew an inch each day. I remember the last day. Remember it so clear. Blue sky morning. I put my hand up there against the sky and thought I could feel how blue it was. It was that blue. A real touchable blue. Thought it might feel like thick water. I waved goodbye to my kid. He took one hand off his bag and did a quick wave. If I wasn't his father I wouldn't've have seen it. You get a sense for those kinds of things. But I was sure of it. The wave. Still am. I can bring it back when I close my eyes. It felt like he wasn't much older than a baby. Felt like he was growing an inch each day. He was a racehorse running for the sun. That day the cop cars raced past my office. There were so many of them. I didn't know the city had so many. They just kept coming. One after another. I knew it like you know a house in the dark after you've lived in it a long time. It just felt like I was moving to another room. The way I got in the car. The way I drove without feeling my feet on the pedals. I saw the yellow tape and the people crying. I knew it, then. But I had known it long before.

I'm sorry, I said.

After it happened, life felt like holding up a bridge from one side only.

An impossible task, I said.

Sure is. Especially when—

And here he stopped, and his eyes glanced briefly at the green notebook beneath the bobbling beagle.

When, I said. When what?

That notebook, he said. Used to be filled with things I clipped out or printed off the web. For a long time I was a mess. Stayed up all night plugging the shooter's name into my computer, seeing what came up. I can close my eyes and see his face. Never seen it in person. Just the small square of it on the big square of my screen.

As he spoke, I thought about that day long ago, sitting on a bench, scrolling through the messages. I thought about the rage and the anger, my name at the heart of it. I thought about how I could throw my phone away and make that part—the part that involved me—disappear. But not all things disappear. When you're escaping one tragedy, sometimes someone else is still at the heart of whatever hurts. There are things that don't leave us, no matter how often we leave, or how far we go. What you carry is no small part of who you are. Invisible burden. Heavy load. This rage or sorrow or anger or grief we call a life.

The grief, I said. It must have been awful.

He was a kid, he said. Fucking just a kid.

Your son, I said.

No, he said. The shooter. Just a fucking kid. And it was late one night. My eyes bugged out from staring at my screen. Reading, just reading. Nonsense words. Radical. Mental. Agenda. Guns.

Assault. Mourn. Tragedy. Never. Again. And I realized I had been thinking more about this kid than my own.

Jesus, I said. I'm so sorry.

And I took that notebook—here, look at it.

And he gave me the notebook with his right hand. Worn thing, a cover hard but still bendable. Forest green but smudged with ink and coffee and oil and more.

And, he said, I ripped out everything I had pasted in there. Go ahead—look.

And I looked. I saw where the pages had been torn away from someone ripping something off of them. And in their place, I saw page after page of this man's handwriting. Each page, its own sentence, scrawled vertically in huge letters from bottom to top:

I am still here, and I will love.

I must carry his memory in place of his life.

Fuck. Fuck! Fuck. It's hard.

I don't need to get over, but I must move forward.

Sometimes one day feels like a year.

My heart is bigger than I believe.

While I live, I must love.

The hard days are not the worst days. The worst days are over.

My heart takes two hands to hold.

Everyone's heart takes two hands to hold.

I walked the trail for a long time after that moment, he said as I read. I walked the hell away from that late night life of reading the whole goddamn internet. That's what it felt like. Walking away from that life. Walking into my own. When I was done, I started doing this. I wanted to be a cornerstone in the lives of others. To be in-between things, holding them up. Not holding up a bridge from just one side. No. Never again.

He paused. The Civic had stopped. It was grunting and humming and lathering the asphalt with spilled gasoline.

We're here, by the way, he said.

I looked up and saw a little notch in one side of the road where the trees spread open. A little notch in the other. I closed the notebook, put it back under the bobbling beagle.

I don't know which way you're going, he said, but I wish you luck. I hope you get wherever you're trying to go.

I don't know if I'm going, I said. Or where. Is that okay?

Is what okay?

Is it okay if I sit here for a second? If I try to figure out something?

Anything, he said.

I unfolded the gas station map and spread it out on the dashboard. I had to lift up the notebook one more time. I had to lift up the bobbling beagle that sat atop it. I placed both back down on the map. I traced my finger along the yellow line.

Can you tell me where we are, I said.

The trail angel leaned forward. His beard, though white, had flecks of burnt yellow, flakes of gold. They dusted the top of the map. He studied the roads and the lines, and then he ran his finger along the paper.

Here, he said. Right here.

His finger stopped at the end of the highlighted path. I looked up, out the window. There was nothing there but the road and the trees that spread open. They were spindly and long and dotted with rocks at their roots, rocks that caught the afternoon's light and shone in the mineral way that rocks shine, like miniature universes. The trees knew there was a trail running between them and they leaned over it and away from it at the same time, providing both cover and space. I thought it was a big world, this one. And wide. I thought it was enough to hold all of us. I didn't know where I would go or what I would do. I would sit for a second. I would figure out what to do with my life. I didn't have to move.

And that's when I saw it, or him. I'm not sure. I'll never be. But the way he came out of the trees, just in front of the car, lanky and long-limbed and flying. One foot touching the ground, then lifting, then the other. As if he was playing a game with himself. Something someone might make up after school, just hanging around with other kids. Something you'd make to pass the time. It was like that. Gentle, fleeting, intangible. You'd miss it if you weren't looking. It was like that. I saw him running across the road. His whole body landing then lifting then flying then landing again. A boy running. I don't know if it was him. But he looked so beautiful. I hope it was.

Acknowledgements

Thank you to my family. To my dad for showing up for me, over and over again. I'll never forget it. You have made my life possible. And to my mom, for being a model of grace and courage, and for gifting me all those books and journals when I was a kid, reminding me that it was good and wonderful to try to be an artist. And to my brother, my first friend and companion, for all the miles we've shared and all that are still to come. And to my late grandmother, and all those long drives to Rochester, which meant more to me than I could ever share. I'm still trying to share.

In her book *Having and Being Had*, Eula Biss writes: "The poets I knew made their money like everyone else, as teachers or bartenders, but what they did for poetry, and for each other, was most often given away." I don't think this book would have ever become *a book* if people hadn't given so much and offered so much to me. Bud Smith, you are the most generous person in literature. Thanks for printing out the first draft of this and marking it up with guitar solos and annotations and edits. You believed in this first, and it helped me believe in it myself. George Kovalenko, thank you for being my friend for all of these years, my ardent idealist, my never-ending conversationalist—your poems and your heart live in this thing. Thanks for offering them to me. Jimmy Cajoleas, you gave so much of your care and your heart into your reading of this when I felt down and out about it. Thanks for giving it life, and giving me life. Krista Stevens, thanks for picking up that first essay at *Longreads* all those years ago, and for editing my work since then, and for saying yes over and over again to my voice—that was a gift. Michael Mungiello, my agent, thanks for not giving up on this novel. And thank you, finally, to Emily Adrian and Alex Higley at Great Place Books for your care and your belief. I'm wildly grateful.

I'm grateful to have so many more people to thank. Absolutely nuts! My best friends, who have run so many miles with me; thank you Nick, Ben, Julian, Matt, and A-Rod for your love, your company, and your companionship. What a joy it is to have friends who drop what they are doing to read some of my words. I feel like Neil Young in *The Last Waltz* when he says *it's one of the joys of my life to be on this stage with these people right now* every time I'm with you.

Thank you to my coworkers and friends at Comp Sci High for teaching with me and letting me learn from you for nearly a decade. Thanks, Logan, for teaching right beside me for five years. There's no intimacy quite like that. Thank you to the grad school writing crew: Katie, George, Brian, Jared, Seth. Thanks especially, George, for writing that little chapbook of poems with me and staying up late together in your backyard so long ago, reading Larry Levis poems back and forth. You won't have to look far to find those nights in this book. Thank you to every reader who read at Dead Rabbits during our tenure (there were hundreds! absolutely wild!), and thank you Katie for planning and running every one of those Sunday nights together, standing with me and listening from behind the bar. Thank you to the community of readers of *Ordinary Plots*. For your emails and your reflections and your own work. Thank you to the writers and editors and poets who have, in one way or another, given so much to me and visited my classrooms and taught me so much else over all these years: Steve, Carlie, Bible, Rax, Kwame, Ariel, Caits, Sasha, Bella, Ron, Maya, Victoria, Maggie, Hannah, Leah, Hanif, Bernard,

Ben, José, and more. The list goes on. I feel so lucky that the list goes on.

I owe the names of some of the characters in this work to poets: Larry Levis, Phil Levine, Sharon Olds. In the joy of writing this novel, I thought it a deeper joy to offer a little homage to such poets, whose work has meant the world. Thank you, you poets, for that.

Thank you to every teacher I've ever had, in classrooms and outside of them. Mr. Rissetto and Professor Greenfield: I'm looking at you. It's funny, sitting here and writing this, I can't help but think that, for all the talk about what we make of ourselves and everything we glamorize about individual effort, such claims are baseless if they ignore the fact that we are held up, each day, by one another and by the ghosts of who we've met and lost along the way. We wear patchwork shirts. We float in leaky boats. We are stitched-together things, repaired as we go on—loved in such a way.

Finally, thank you, Meg, for being my first reader and editor, and for teaching me all that you have about grace, empathy for our future selves, and love. One of the first things you ever told me was that you read the acknowledgments of a book before you begin it, so hello there. I'm saving the best for last.

Great Place Books publishes literary fiction, nonfiction, poetry, and work in translation. Our mission is to be a home for rigorous, weird, beautiful books—and their readers. These books are imperiled by the stratification and commercialization of publishing. Against the grain of the industry and the times, we aim to support the careers of idiosyncratic and alluring writers whose voices might otherwise be lost.

www.greatplacebooks.com